DESERT RAILS

DESERT RAILS

L. P. Holmes

Chivers Press   •   **Thorndike Press**
Bath, England   **Waterville, Maine USA**

This Large Print edition is published by Chivers Press, England, and by Thorndike Press, USA.

Published in 2003 in the U.K. by arrangement with the author c/o Golden West Literary Agency.

Published in 2003 in the U.S. by arrangement with Golden West Literary Agency.

U.K. Hardcover   ISBN 0–7540–8943–6 (Chivers Large Print)
U.K. Softcover   ISBN 0–7540–8944–4 (Camden Large Print)
U.S. Softcover   ISBN 0–7862–4919–6 (Nightingale Series)

The text of this Large Print edition is unabridged.
Other aspects of the book may vary from the original edition.

Set in 16 pt. New Times Roman.

Printed in Great Britain on acid-free paper.

British Library Cataloguing in Publication Data available

Library of Congress Cataloging-in-Publication Data

Holmes, L. P. (Llewellyn Perry), 1895–
    Desert rails / by L.P. Holmes.
       p.   cm.
    ISBN 0–7862–4919–6 (lg. print : sc : alk. paper)
    1. Railroads—Design and construction—Fiction. 2. Large type
books. I. Title.
PS3515.O4448 D47 2003
813'.52—dc21
                                   2002036016

CHAPTER ONE

TROUBLESHOOTER

The northern approach to Rockaway Pass was a steady, steam-eating grind and by the time the four-car, narrow-gauge freight train topped out at Kicking Horse, the little Simcoe engine up ahead was glad to pull in at the water tower for a refill of the tender tank.

Back in the caboose the brakeman left off talking to the girl in gray and hurried out as the engine whistled the stop. The girl stood up, moved over to a small, dusty window and stood there, looking out across the lonely sagebrush hills of the high Nevada desert. Guardedly, Luke Fenimore watched her.

She was fairly tall, with an easy, erect grace. Her hair was ebony black, her eyes a clear, flawless gray, a contrast as startling as it was effective. There was a certain molded warmth about her mouth and chin which softened and shaded her profile just enough to balance the high, bright pride reflected there. She was definitely the handsomest girl Luke Fenimore had ever seen and it was hard to keep his eyes off her. That she was conscious of Luke's regard, and resented it, showed when she turned her head abruptly and faced him fully, a cold disdain coming into her eyes.

Luke started a trifle guiltily, then shrugged, touching his hat. 'I'm sorry,' he said gravely. 'I meant no offence. But beauty was made to be looked at.'

He turned and started toward the rear of the platform of the caboose, only to find the way blocked as three men came pushing in. They moved with a rough swaggering and Luke, drawing on the wisdom of past observation, classed them as mule skinners. He paused, waiting for them to make way and let him pass. They showed no intention of doing this. Instead, they fanned out three abreast, effectively blocking off the little car.

A thread of bright, hard alertness ran through Fenimore, sharpening his eyes, bringing him slightly up on his toes, balanced and ready. It was a move purely instinctive on his part. His voice was quiet but curt as he asked, 'Looking for somebody, maybe?'

'That's right,' answered the middle one of the three. 'We are. For a man named Fenimore.' There was a cocksure belligerence to this fellow.

'You've found him,' said Luke. 'So now—?'

'Why,' was the reply, 'this is where you get off. You've changed your mind. You're not going on to Cold Creek. You're getting off here and hitting the ties back to Garnet. When you get there you can let your conscience be your guide, just so long as it points you east, west or north. But not south again. Get it? Not

2

south.'

A faintly slurring note came into Luke Fenimore's tone, almost a drawl. 'And if I decide not to get off?'

'Oh, but you will. That's what the three of us are here for, to see that you do. Come on, now—don't let's have any fuss over something that's already decided. Off you get!'

Luke Fenimore was thirty years old. Behind him lay a good dozen years of experience in the ways of rough, tough camps and rough, tough men. Contact with such elements had inevitably toughened him. It had also taught him a great deal. Among other things it had taught him that when trouble or conflict loomed and had to be faced, then the safest course and the one most promising of success was to meet a challenge headlong and for keeps. He had learned that attack, as overwhelming and ruthless as possible, plus surprise, was far better than any defense. Also he had learned, when the odds were three to one, that only a fool was held down by any fancy rules. Against such odds a smart man used any means that came to hand with which to smash and disable.

So now, as he measured these three and read their purpose, Luke loosened his shoulders with a slight shrug and murmured, with a deeper meaning than any of the three guessed, 'If I must, I must.'

A little behind Luke and to his right, resting

on the bench which ran along the side of the caboose, was his sum total of baggage. It was a small, badly scuffed, stained old canvas-sided gripsack. It looked harmless and innocent enough, but only Luke knew that tucked deep within it, right against the very bottom of it, were several pounds of hard, unyielding metal, in the shape of a heavy Colt revolver, holstered and wrapped around by a cartridge belt. Also, there was a full, unbroken box of ammunition for that gun.

Luke's first move in reaching for his gripsack was natural and completely disarming. His next was savage and explosive. For, with the half turn of his body and the stretch of his arm as leverage, he brought the gripsack forward in a half sweep, half throw, driving it full into the face of the spokesman of the three. The crunch of impact was solid, wicked. The fellow went down as though hit with a sledge hammer. The odds had been cut down by a full third.

Luke let the impetus of the throw carry him forward, and he drove into the second tough before the fellow could fully get his guard up. Luke carried his man back along the car, ripping both fists into the fellow's face—hard, chopping, damaging blows. Back, Luke drove him, back until he crashed into the corner of the caboose, and there Luke held him, putting everything he had into his pumping, thudding fists. He dug one deep into the fellow's body, brought him over gasping and sick. Then Luke aimed for the nerve on the side of the neck, up under the ear. It was a clean shot and it brought the fellow down, loose and sprawling. The solid shock of that last punch told Luke that now the odds were even.

None of this had taken very long and Luke had never stopped moving, using every split second of his surprise advantage to the best end possible, for he knew there would be a price to be paid before this thing was finished. The first element of surprise and explosive action was done with and his back was to the third tough.

He knew what was coming, so now he crouched low as he whirled, dropping his head and wrapping his arms protectively about it. He was barely in time. Flailing, savage blows clubbed at him. The curtain of his arms helped Luke some, but could not ward off all of the blows. One smashed against the side of his head, another thudded down on the back of his neck, close up against the skull. It was a rabbit punch that hurt and shook Luke up badly. But Luke bored in, still low and crouched, knowing that he had to take it until he could get in close.

Those smashing fists beat down at the broad of Luke's shoulders, rabbit-punched him again and again. A paralyzing numbness began to tighten through Luke and he realized that another solid rabbit punch would put him down. So he gathered his feet under him and drove forward, smashing a shoulder into the tough's legs. The shock sent the fellow staggering backward, but it also dropped Luke to his hands and knees.

He lunged up, dove forward again. This time he got hold of the fellow's belt and, despite another battering of blows about the head, dragged himself close and got his arms about the tough's waist. Then with his feet spread for the lift and leverage he needed, Luke sank the point of his shoulder into his adversary's stomach, half lifted him from his feet, whirled him around and carried him crashing into the side of the car. As that barrier abruptly stopped the fellow's backward movement, Luke rolled his hunched shoulder forward with all the drive and weight he had.

It was like an extra-savage blow to the solar plexus and it wrung a grunt from the man. Luke jerked him away from the caboose wall, hurled him back into it again using another shot of that shoulder punishment. And this time, with a gust of savage satisfaction, Luke could feel the betraying looseness that came over the man. Luke gave him the shoulder treatment for a third time, then stepped back, entirely clear, letting his man sag forward, wickedly hurt and weakening.

When you had been through this sort of thing before, many times, Luke thought, you came to know when you had your man where you wanted him, when all the fight had been completely knocked out of him and he was ripe for the finish. So now Luke set himself, sighted for that half-open, sagging jaw and hit it savagely. His fist and wrist went a trifle numb and again the solid shock of the punch came up his arm and cushioned in the heavy muscles of his shoulder and back. The man jerked sideways and collapsed.

Less than thirty seconds had ticked by from the first to the last of this thing, but they had been wild, explosive seconds that took much out of a man. So now Luke was content to lean a supporting hand against the caboose wall, while he gulped hoarsely for breath and shook the numbing fog out of his brain. Those rabbit punches hadn't done him any good at all.

He was dimly conscious of the girl in gray standing at the forward end of the caboose, shocked and still, one slim hand at her throat. Luke managed a twisted grin. 'Rough business,' he croaked. 'But then, it's a rough country.'

He retrieved his gripsack, put it back on the side bench. Then, one by one he dragged the three out to the rear platform of the caboose and tumbled them down into the sage by the right of way. The one he had hit with the gripsack was still out cold. The other two were beginning to regain their scattered wits, but showed no disposition to carry this thing further, or to argue over their none too gentle ejection from the train. Luke had just finished getting rid of the last of them when the brakeman came back to the caboose, to stare in wide-eyed amazement.

'What's been going on here?' he demanded.

Luke shrugged. 'Those three hard cases climbed into the caboose with the idea of throwing me off and starting me back to Garnet. Just why, I haven't even a thin guess. Naturally, I objected. They seem to have changed their minds on the matter.'

The brakeman looked over the three with a callous eye, then shrugged. 'They've been hanging around here at Kicking Horse for the past week. Every time we stopped for water on the southbound run, they'd come in out of the sage and take a look in the caboose. I braced them on the idea and they said they were waiting for a friend who was to meet them here. And you were him, eh?'

'Hardly a friend,' Luke drawled. 'Truth is, I never saw any of them before in my life. Well, they won't have to hang around on that chore any longer.'

Up ahead the Simcoe sent the wail of its whistle echoing across the lonely sage. The couplings took up with a jerk and the wheels began to turn. The brakeman hopped nimbly aboard. 'I've seen that one with the bushy eyebrows and crooked nose skinning a freight outfit for Jack Fargo. What would Fargo be having against you?'

'I wouldn't know,' shrugged Luke. 'I don't know him either.'

The brakeman looked back at the three men beside the track, one of them still lying prone. 'After that you probably will. Jack Fargo was never one to be bashful about walkin' down the middle of the street with big, wide steps. Well, it's none of my pie.'

With this the brakeman went on into the caboose with the obvious intention of taking up his conversation with the girl in gray. In this he was doomed to quick disappointment, for the girl's mood was one of such reserved, distant preoccupation that the brakeman soon took the hint and subsided. After which he did considerable disgruntled staring at Luke, as though he felt that in some way Luke was to blame for his discomfiture.

As for Luke, he settled quietly back on the bench, immersed in his own thoughts. From time to time he absently fingered the back of his neck and one side of his face, where the darkness of a bruise was beginning to take shape. Now it was the girl who several times stole sober, guarded glances at the quietly thoughtful man across the caboose from her. But presently, when Luke stirred and reached for his pipe, she swung her eyes quickly away and did not look at him again.

*　　　*　　　*

9

The rail-end town of Cold Creek was sprawling, raw-boarded and ugly. Luke Fenimore was neither impressed nor disappointed at what he saw. For in his time he had seen a lot of rough construction-camp towns and there was a certain sameness to all of them. They seldom achieved permanence. They grew quickly, they died quickly. And beauty was never in any of them.

The drifting wail of the Simcoe's whistle had signaled approach to the town and the girl in gray had gone immediately back to the platform of the caboose, waiting there almost impatiently for the little train to roll to a halt. As soon as it did she swung lithely down the steps and walked swiftly away. Luke Fenimore reached the platform to see the brakeman staring wistfully after her.

'There ought,' said the brakie, 'to be a law against a girl as pretty as her moving through a world of lonely men. I dunno what Bart Runnell ever did to deserve such luck.'

'I wouldn't know about that,' said Luke dryly. 'But maybe you can tell me where to locate Ma Megarry's boardinghouse?'

'Sure,' said the brakie. 'It's the only two-story building on the left side of the street. About halfway up.'

A pale thin sunlight was beginning to work timidly through the midday overcast. The early spring air still had a raw bite to it, the lingering breath of a late departing winter. In some of

10

the hollows of the rolling sage hills beyond the town, a faint powdering of snow still clung.

Half a dozen big freight-wagon outfits were pulled up beside the railroad track and from them men were laboriously unloading heavy gray lead ingots. Still farther along, beyond the southern edge of town, were a number of huge corrals holding the shifting, living mass of score upon score of mules. Pulled up in line around the corrals, empty freight wagons loomed like clumsy, uncouth giants at rest. All these things Luke Fenimore took in with a speculative sweep of his eyes, before heading uptown.

He located the boardinghouse without difficulty and when he entered was faced by a brawny Irishwoman with twinkling eyes and a rich, slurring brogue. She said, 'I'm Ma Megarry. You're wishin' lodgings maybe, Mister?'

Luke nodded. 'If you have them. Joe Keller recommended your place to me, Mrs. Megarry. My name is Fenimore, Luke Fenimore.'

'Well, now,' said Ma Megarry genially, 'if you're a friend of Joe Keller, why then you're a friend of mine. Come along.'

The second-story room was small, but neat and clean. 'Dinner has been over a full hour past,' Ma Megarry said. 'But if you'd be after likin' a meal, then I think a bite or two can be found in the kitchen.'

Luke shook his head, smiling. 'I'll wait until supper. Just now I want to clean up a bit and then have a look around.'

'And will you be after goin' to work for John Guthrie?' probed Ma Megarry.

'For John Guthrie,' admitted Luke. 'I had a long talk with him at Garnet. I'm to be the new Grade Superintendent.'

'Ha!' exclaimed Ma Megarry. 'And are you now! That's news which my own Johnny boy will be glad to hear. We were talking of that very thing at breakfast this morning, my Johnny and I, and it was Johnny himself who said that if something wasn't done pretty soon about getting a real man in place of that drunken, blustering, worthless Bole Ives, why then there never would be enough new grade cut to lay Mr. Guthrie's railroad on. But'—and here the kindly Irishwoman's eyes showed a glint of worry—'there'll likely be trouble ahead for you, Ma. Luke. It was my Johnny who said as much.'

Luke smiled again. 'That will be taken care of, too. Is your Johnny with the grade gang?'

'With the very same, Mr. Luke. And if there are other things you might want to know about the gang, Johnny can tell you.'

'I could use a little more information,' admitted Luke. 'John Guthrie gave me some of the picture, but it generally takes one of the men of the gang to know the real undercurrents and what causes them. I'd like to talk to your Johnny.'

Ma Megarry stepped into the hall and sent a call echoing through the building, to which there came a rumbling reply and then the solid, measured tread of a big man, coming up the stairs.

Johnny Megarry was a young giant, with tremendous shoulders, arms like the limbs of a tree and with a blunt jaw and a fine, slightly frowning steadiness about his eyes which Luke liked immediately.

Said Ma Megarry, 'Johnny, shake hands with Mr. Luke Fenimore, who is replacing that worthless Bole Ives. There'll be things he'll want to know about the grade gang and it is you who can tell him. And when he goes down to the bunkhouses to lay the law down to some of those loafers, do you go along with him and see to it that they don't gang up on him.'

Johnny Megarry's huge fist fairly swallowed Luke's own sinewy hand. 'Hah!' he rumbled. 'And this is the best news I've heard since the snow quit fallin'. It is happy I am to know you, Mr. Fenimore, and I'll be glad to help you any way I can.'

'Then sit down on that bunk and talk to me while I clean up,' said Luke, stripping off his short, fleece-lined coat.

Ma Megarry went out and Luke peeled off his blue woolen shirt, went over to the battered bureau, poured water from the big white pitcher into its companion bowl. Johnny

Megarry lowered his huge bulk onto the edge of the bunk and gave Luke a long, measuring survey, nodding his head in silent approval at what he saw.

Luke Fenimore stood just a shade under six feet. His waist was lean and narrow and compact and there was a swelling depth and breadth to his chest and shoulders. His features were rugged, his skin a weathered brown, with a firm, tough, well-scrubbed look to it. Halfway between the line of his vigorous, slightly unruly brown hair and his left eyebrow, there was a shadow of an old scar, with another of the same at one corner of his long, firm lips. His eyes were a cool, clear blue which saw much yet revealed little, except perhaps to mirror a faint, slightly sardonic skepticism. It was the look of a man who believed in himself and trusted himself, but who was somewhat wary of including others too deeply in this confidence; the look of a man pretty well committed to the lone-wolf theory of existence.

Johnny Megarry said, 'Any time you wish, Mr. Fenimore, I'll be glad to take you down and introduce you to the boys of the grade gang. And I'd like to say right now that aside from one or two of them, they're not at all a bad bunch, when you get to know them. It is the gang I work with myself, so I know them well. This mite of trouble is not all their fault. It's just that of late, since the rumor has been around that Bole Ives was on the way out, there has been no head or tail to things, what with Bole Ives sulkin' and drinkin', and with Cob Ogard, the foreman, mule-sore because his friend Ives is by way of bein' fired. Then Bart Runnell, the over-all Construction Super, he's been away on some kind of business and there just seems to be nobody who really knows what from which. And when things get that way, Mr. Fenimore, you know how things go with a gang.'

Luke nodded. 'I know, Johnny. A construction gang is like a ship. It gets nowhere unless there is someone on hand to steer it. This Cob Ogard? John Guthrie seems to feel that he's not too good an influence with the other men. What do you think?'

The frown deepened about Johnny Megarry's eyes. 'I'm not one to carry tales, Mr. Fenimore, unless I feel that it is my duty to do so for the sake of the job. So I'll say this of Cob Ogard—the man is a troublemaker. He's a wicked fighter and the men fear him, but they do not like him. If I were in John Guthrie's boots, then I would fire Cob Ogard as well as Bole Ives and know that the gang would be all the better for it.'

Luke Fenimore dove into the cold luxury of the water, splashing it about his face and neck. It struck and soothed the stiffness of the bruises forming there and Luke felt much his normal self when he toweled himself

15

vigorously. He grinned at Johnny Megarry.

'You've made up my mind for me, Johnny. Cob Ogard goes!'

Johnny nodded. 'I figured it so, Mr. Fenimore. But I must warn you. Cob Ogard will not fire easily. I have said he is a wicked fighter. I say it again. He'll cause you trouble. He'll be sure to challenge you, and you'll have to fight him and whip him to win the respect of the gang.'

Luke laughed softly. 'A condition I've bumped into before, Johnny. So far I have always managed somehow. We won't worry about it. And now about the job itself. How are we fixed for tools? Can't cut grade without tools, you know.'

'We've the tools,' declared Johnny. 'And the men who know how to use them. We're well fixed that way. It is only the spirit and organization we're lacking. If you bring those two things with you, why then no one will be able to find fault with our progress.'

'The country ahead of us—grade levels and things of that sort—what about them?'

Johnny Megarry laughed ruefully. 'Now you are getting way over my head, Mr. Fenimore. At my best I am still just a grade-gang jerry. I can cut right of way to grade stakes, but for the levels and the figuring which goes into them, why, you'll have to see young Dick Leslie, who is our engineer. And a fine boy Dick is. Smart as a whip and with all his heart in the job. If

16

you would see him, you'll more than likely find him at the cabin where he and his sister live. I can point it out to you from this window.'

Luke ran a comb through his hair and picked up his hat. 'Which cabin, Johnny?'

Johnny showed him and, as they left the room, Luke said, 'I'll see you at the bunkhouses in the morning, Johnny. Then we will find out about this Cob Ogard—and other things.'

Luke made his way across town to the Leslie cabin, which managed to achieve a sort of quaint and quiet dignity by standing somewhat apart from the rest of the town. There was a neatness about it, with the flutter of colored curtains at the windows.

Luke knocked at the door and a moment later was standing startled and very still. For the door was opened by the girl who had ridden in the caboose with him from Garnet, the girl in gray. She was in gingham, now—spick and span. She looked younger, more girlish.

Luke fumbled at his hat. 'I understood that Dick Leslie lived here,' he said. 'I wanted to talk with him about railroad business. I'm Luke Fenimore, the new Grade Superintendent.'

She nodded, entirely matter-of-fact. 'Won't you come in? I'll call Dick.'

Her voice was low and rich. At her call a slender young fellow in laced boots, corduroy trousers and gray flannel shirt came in. His face was sensitive, handsome, but with a hint of grimness about the mouth. There were inkstains on his fingers and he was carrying a draftsman's pencil.

'This is Mr. Fenimore, Dick,' said the girl. 'The rumor that Bole Ives was to be let go is true, it seems. For Mr. Fenimore says he is the new Grade Superintendent. He wants to talk to you.'

Dick Leslie's smile was quick and genuine as he put out his hand. 'Glad to know you, Fenimore. This is great news—that we've got rid of Bole Ives at last. Certainly high time. Er—this is my sister, Dale.'

Luke met the impersonal reserve of the girl's glance, inclined his head and murmured, 'My very good fortune, Miss Leslie.' He turned back to the brother. 'Hope I'm not bothering you too much, but there are some angles of this job I'd like to talk over with you.'

'Tickled to death,' was the hearty reply. 'I've just been checking over some of my figures. Come on into the cubby I call my office when I'm at home.'

It was a small room, crowded with a drafting table, a rack of blueprints, a couple of shelves of engineering books, a stool and a chair. Dick Leslie perched on the stool, waved Luke to the chair. 'Shoot!' he said boyishly.

'First, what's ahead?' asked Luke. 'The country, I mean?'

18

Dick Leslie spread a piece of paper on the table and the pencil in his practiced fingers flew. 'Here is Cold Creek and here is Castle Mountain. Our right of way leads along the valley of the Castle River. We will have to cross the river four times. A great deal of the year Castle River is just a spread of alkali-whitened rocks and gravel. The rest of the time it is anything from a trickle of dirty water to a hell-raising, wild-eyed flood. So, while holding our gradients to a minimum, we must allow enough to be sure we'll be above maximum level of any flood water that may come along. Even so, all the worst of our elevations are behind us, thanks be! From here on in to Castle Mountain it would be all clear sailing if it wasn't—' Young Leslie paused.

'If it wasn't—what?' prodded Luke.

'Why,' explained the young engineer soberly, 'if it wasn't that we have to beat that subsidy deadline. The rest doesn't amount to a hoot, unless we can beat that deadline. You've heard of it, of course?'

'A little,' Luke admitted. 'John Guthrie mentioned it. Quite a chunk of money at stake, I understand.'

'Just a cool quarter of a million,' said Dick Leslie. 'State money, of course. The powers that be at Carson City are pretty stern about this subsidy, for which you can't rightfully blame them. For on a couple of past occasions at which they voted an outright subsidy

19

without a definite time limit, some shady promoters took advantage, using up all the money and skipping with fat profits, but never actually finishing the railroad which they started and leaving it up to the state to gather the loose ends and finish the job with a lot of added expense. So, the state very definitely doesn't intend letting anything like that happen on this job. In fact, they're not allowing us any comfortable leeway at all. Which is ironic, to say the least. For this is one railroad where the men backing it are acting in entire good faith. You've computed the time and distance we are up against?'

Luke nodded. 'Forty-five miles in thirty-four days. Roughly a mile and a third of steel to go down each day. No time for woolgathering, I'll admit. But it can be done, with reasonable organization and effort. I've been on jobs where standard steel went down faster than that. This layout is narrow gauge, which means handling thirty-five-pound steel against ninety- or hundred-pound. Roughly, we'll be grading for a three-foot track instead of a five-foot. That same two-foot margin holds good on bridges and culverts, and figures in on side clearance in cuts. The mine interests in Castle Mountain are backing the road, I understand.'

'That's right. Henry Shard, Frank Ames and Curtis Leffingwell. They own the lead mines and smelters at Castle Mountain. They've borrowed to the hilt against that subsidy and unless we put a train inside the town limits of Castle Mountain by midnight of May 30th next, those three men will lose their shirts.'

'I think we can do that and maybe have a little time to spare,' said Luke.

'I hope so,' Dick Leslie said soberly. 'There would be no slightest cause for us to worry and run a temperature over this thing if everything were going well in the way of organization and if we had everything we need. But right now, in the way of rolling stock, we have one Simcoe engine, half a dozen boxcars and a dozen flats. The Simcoe is worked to death. It has to haul lead pigs from Cold Creek out to Garnet, on the main transcontinental line, and bring back not only all the supplies we need but what Castle Mountain and the mines need as well.

'Then there is Jack Fargo, whose freight wagons fill in the gap between Cold Creek and Castle Mountain. Fargo has right around fifty wagons on the road all the time, going and coming. He's got close to six hundred mules. These mules eat a lot of hay and grain, which we also have to haul in from Garnet. Alec Craigie and Casey O'Keefe have done wonders in keeping the Simcoe rolling, but we can't count on wonders forever. If the Simcoe ever does have a major breakdown, we're whipped, for time is the one thing we can't afford to waste and which we can't bring back, once it is gone. Finally, there is steel.'

Something in the way Dick Leslie added this

last made Luke's head jerk up. 'What about steel?' he asked sharply.

Dick Leslie shrugged. 'We may run short of it.'

Luke hit his feet, took a short turn up and down the room. His voice took on a curt, cold ring. 'What kind of a layout is this Desert & Central Railroad, anyhow? I knew there was a mess in the grade gang which has to be straightened out. That will be done, first thing tomorrow morning. I knew there were several other angles which were more or less held together by a shoestring. But I didn't know they were trying to build a railroad without steel. For steel is the foundation, the payoff to everything. You can figure a temporary answer to about everything else. But steel you must have! What's the answer to a shortage of the stuff at this time?'

Dick Leslie shook a reluctant head. 'I'm not sure enough in my information to supply the entire answer. But for one thing it seems the mills are going to be a little slow on delivery. Right now we are plenty short, in such a pinch that Bart Runnell is away, trying to line up some secondhand steel, perhaps enough to keep us going until the new stuff arrives from the mills. Let's hope he gets it!'

Luke took another turn or two across the little room. So this was it! Steel—or rather, lack of it. Just another weak link in a chain loosely put together. Now he was able to put a

22

finger on an almost impalpable something, an atmosphere, which he had sensed right from the first. He had sensed it in his talk with John Guthrie, back at Garnet. He had sensed it in Joe Keller, who had been at Garnet with Guthrie. He had sensed it in big, slow-speaking, steadfastly honest Johnny Megarry. And he had sensed it in this young engineer in front of him now, Dick Leslie.

In all of them lay a sort of blindly dogged determination, but also a gnawing doubt. They were men set to try and fight a job through, while all the time, deep down within them, was a growing conviction that they were going to lose, that they weren't going to make that subsidy deadline. And the reason was a sort of distrust in organization, in supplies, in all the vital things necessary to build and keep on building until the job was licked.

Luke hadn't been able exactly to place that nagging atmosphere at first. But he could now. And he could see the reason. He laughed a trifle harshly. 'Looks like I've stuck my neck out,' he said bluntly. 'Like I was a sucker to leave the job I had to come and take over this one. I could almost get sore at Guthrie. There were things he could have told me, but didn't.'

Dick Leslie was watching him, sober and worried. 'Hope I haven't talked too much,' said the young engineer. 'But you asked for the picture and I've given it to you as honestly as I know how. Whatever you do, Fenimore, don't

23

hold anything against John Guthrie. He's eating his heart out about this job. It means so much to him to put it over. It isn't his fault that things are not all that they should be. I know that he has never stopped working and begging and arguing for the things we need.'

Luke shrugged and dropped back into his chair. 'Don't know why I should worry about steel,' he growled, as though speaking a thought aloud. 'My job is to build grade and I'll see that that is done, at any rate.'

While they had talked, the afternoon had run away. Now the gloom of early evening was outside and the lights went on in other rooms of the cabin. Then it was Dale Leslie who was in the doorway, saying, 'You two have talked enough to build a thousand miles of railroad. Supper is ready.'

Luke jumped up, reaching for his hat. 'Good Lord! I had no idea—! Miss Leslie, I beg your pardon. You should have thrown me out, long ago.'

For the first time her cool reserve softened just a trifle. The faintest of smiles touched her lips. 'I've set a place for you, too. It's a relief to have someone around for Dick to talk job to, someone who really understands what he is driving at. Which I, frankly, do not. Though I listen the best I can, for I know how much it means to Dick.'

'It's my first big job,' said Dick Leslie simply. 'It just has to be right. My whole future

24

can depend on it.'

It was the most pleasant meal Luke Fenimore had sat down to in a long, long time. Behind him lay a succession of third-rate boom-town hotels, of hash houses, of boardinghouses and construction-camp cook shacks. Here in this neat little cabin was white napery and gleaming tableware.

By no slightest sign did Luke show how acutely conscious he was of the girl who sat across the table from him. The light of the hanging lamp built up bright, metallic glints in her hair, and laid soft shadows about her chin and throat. Her every move held a lithe, smooth grace and her soft, rich voice was melody in the ears of a lonely man. Luke remembered how she had caught him watching her in the caboose of the train on the trip in from Garnet, and also the cool disdain she had shown in return. He did not want to risk another rebuff. So careful was he of this, he unconsciously laid a shell of remoteness about him which caused both of the Leslies to throw wondering glances at him.

Through the early night the bay of a whistle sounded. 'That's Alec Craigie and Casey O'Keefe, back from Garnet again,' exclaimed Dick Leslie. 'The hardest-working engine crew in the world, those two. I don't know what we'd do without them. To hear them rawhide each other you'd think they were always on the brink of breaking into mortal combat. But start a fight with one and you have both of them on your neck. Wonder if they bring any news from Bart, Sis?'

Luke, recalling the remark made by the brakeman on the arrival of the train at Cold Creek, glanced at Dale Leslie. Her head was up, her eyes shining. She seemed to be listening.

It didn't make a lick of sense, but something went out of the evening for Luke Fenimore, right then and there. The brakie had mentioned this girl along with Bart Runnell. Now, when her brother mentioned the possibility of Runnell coming in on this trip of the train, the girl was fairly glowing.

A hint of the old sardonic mockery and skepticism came back into Luke's eyes, as though he was inwardly jeering at some momentary sentimental weakness of his own. He wished he was back in his own room at Ma Megarry's boardinghouse. That was the proper place for a lone wolf to be—in his own den.

Luke was glad when the meal was finished. He said, 'There is an old saying about eating and running, Miss Leslie, but I've things to do. It has been very generous of you to have me to supper. It meant more than you imagine. And I thank—'

Luke broke off, abruptly aware that the girl wasn't even listening, at least not to him. For there was the sound of quick approaching steps outside and her eyes were on the door, bright and eager. She fairly flew to answer the knock and her voice was throaty as she cried, 'Bart!'

This fellow Bart Runnell was a big man with square shoulders. He seemed to fill the doorway as he stood there, holding both of the girl's hands while looking down at her. He said, 'Dale! Girl, you look good to me!'

Luke had the feeling that if he and Dick Leslie had not been there, Runnell would have taken Dale Leslie in his arms and that she would not have objected.

Luke was bleak and restless. He wanted to get out of here. But now Bart Runnell was looking across the room and saying, 'Hi, Dick! How are all the little survey stakes?'

'They're all right.' Dick Leslie's voice was slightly tense. 'How about that Grasshopper steel?'

'No luck. Somebody beat us to it.'

'That,' said Dick Leslie slowly, 'is bad.'

Runnell shrugged. 'Breaks of the game. Secondhand steel is miserable stuff to handle, anyhow.'

'Secondhand steel,' retorted Dick Leslie grimly, 'is so much better than no steel at all, it isn't even funny. Where do we go from here, now that we've missed out on that Grasshopper deal?'

Runnell shrugged again. 'That's Guthrie's worry, not mine. He's the big boss. Don't believe I've met your friend.'

27

Dick Leslie said, 'Shake hands with Luke Fenimore, our new Grade Superintendent. Fenimore—Bart Runnell.'

Runnell's glance bored at Luke as they struck hands. 'So Guthrie finally decided to let Bole Ives go, eh? I knew he'd had the idea in his mind for some time. Too bad about Ives. He was a good man until the liquor got him. There's nothing wrong with the grade gang that a little quiet talking to won't cure. I'll drop around to the bunkhouses in the morning with you, Fenimore, and straighten things out.'

'Thanks,' said Luke dryly. 'But I'd rather handle it myself. That's the job I was hired to do.'

'Being a stranger, you won't have all of the picture,' said Runnell, a slightly heavy note coming into his voice. 'You might be mistaken about some of the men, and that would do more harm than good.'

'The harm,' Luke said bluntly, looking Runnell straight in the eye, 'seems to have been done already—before I ever showed up. Now I'll handle things as I think best.'

A flush climbed across Runnell's face, darkening it. 'As superintendent over all construction, I can't risk having a stranger make a mess of one of my gangs.'

'As I get the picture,' retorted Luke curtly, 'the trouble in the grade gang is not just a recent thing, but something that has been brewing for a long time. So I can't help but

28

wonder, now that you seem so concerned, why you didn't scotch it long ago. But you didn't, so now I'm going to.'

Something had come into this quiet, homey little room, a clash of wills, of personalities. The current flowed back and forth between these two men, between Luke Fenimore and Bartley Runnell a current that was full of a quickening bitterness and challenge.

'I said you didn't have all the picture.' That heavy note in Runnell's tone deepened to a growling but guarded truculence. 'So maybe I better put you right on certain matters and settle one point for good and all. I told you, Fenimore, that I was over-all Construction Superintendent. And as such, you and the other gang bosses are directly responsible to me and my orders. I don't want to get tough about it, but that is the way it will have to be. And my orders to you are that you—'

'Save it!' cut in Luke brusquely. 'I'm responsible to just one man—John Guthrie. That was the understanding I had with Guthrie before I took the job. If you feel differently about it, you can hash that out with him. For the present, I'll run my gang my own way and ask help from you and others only if and when I feel I need it. Dick—Miss Leslie, I'll be running along. Thanks again for your hospitality.'

As he stepped past Runnell to the door, Luke flashed a quick glance at Dick Leslie,

29

another at the girl. Dick looked troubled, but his good night was pleasant and friendly. There was a faint flush in the girl's cheeks, however, and her eyes were sparkling with anger. Her parting nod to Luke was barely perceptible.

As the door closed behind Luke and he started off through the night, he muttered, 'She's more than fond of that fellow Runnell, and all torched up at me because I put him back on his heels a little. Well, what of it? This is no time in my young life to start woolgathering just because I've met up with a pretty girl.'

Which was a good, hardheaded conclusion—had it worked. But as he lay in his blankets in his room in Ma Megarry's boardinghouse, Luke found sleep eluding him, as his thoughts went back again and again to Dale Leslie. And before he finally did manage to drop off, Luke came to the realization that forgetting Dale Leslie was going to shape up as the hardest chore he had ever known.

CHAPTER TWO

GANG BOSS

When Luke Fenimore went down to breakfast
the next morning he found at the table, among
others, Joe Keller, the steel boss, Johnny
Megarry, and the engine crew of the Simcoe,
Alec Craigie and Casey O'Keefe. Craigie was
angular and rawboned, with rusty hair and
Scotch blue eyes. Casey O'Keefe, his fireman,
was a solid chunk of Ireland, gay and
impudent and irrepressible. But even Casey
O'Keefe was inclined to soberness at the
moment. About all four of these men was an
air of detached waiting, of suspended
expectations.

It was Casey who finally blurted, 'Alec and
me, we're wonderin' should we hook on an
extra flat to carry the grade gang out to end of
steel, Mr. Fenimore. Or is it going to be like it
has been for the past week, with the grade
gang sprawling on their lazy backs in the
bunkhouses?'

'They'll be going out to work,' Luke told
him quietly. 'The start will be a bit late,
perhaps, for they may take a mite of
convincing. But they'll be going out.'

Casey O'Keefe said, 'Hah!' in obvious
satisfaction, then flashed a triumphant look at

31

Alec Craigie, as though to say, 'I told you so!'

Johnny Megarry stirred uneasily and blurted, 'You'll not be eating too heavily, Mr. Fenimore. For someone has taken the word to the bunkhouses and Cob Ogard is making his boasts.'

'He's a tough one, Ogard is,' said Alec Craigie, in his dry, precise way. 'And there is no such thing as fair fighting in him. You'll be remembering that, Mr. Fenimore.'

'He can be whipped one way,' offered Casey O'Keefe eagerly. 'Now if you can handle your maulies clean-like—hit and get away, I mean—why then you'll be after havin' a fair chance wid him Mr. Fenimore. But if you let him get in close, which is how he likes it, where he can gouge and tear and stomp, why then he can be bad, very bad. For though you are a well-set-up chunk of a man in your own right, I'd say offhand that Ogard will outweigh you some. Besides which, he is strong as a bull.'

Joe Keller said gravely, 'I don't think too many of the men would hold it against you, Fenimore, if you took a pick handle to him. Just so you put him down and keep him there, and show that you're ready to give any of the rest of them the same medicine if they want it that way. If I know that gang—and I think I do—methods won't count much, but results will—definitely.'

A tight grin thinned Luke's lips as he looked around at them all. They made him think of a group of small boys on a school ground, gathering anxiously about their favorite and offering him advice against the trial ahead.

'You boys don't seem to be enjoying your breakfasts the way you should. Ma Megarry's cooking is entirely too good to waste. So relax and quit worrying,' advised Luke. 'I've met several Cob Ogards in my time,' he went on. 'I think I know the type. So I'll probably do all right. Just so you keep any other too ambitious ones off my back when I'm not looking.'

Johnny Megarry flexed his huge paws. 'In that you can depend on me, Mr. Fenimore. That you can!'

'Thanks, Johnny. And now is a good time to drop this mister business. Make it plain Luke. I answer best that way, and that's the way I like it.'

Luke ate well, but not too heavily, packed and lighted his pipe and was ready to go. They went out and down the street in a little group. The first person they met was Dick Leslie, who fell into step with Luke. Dick looked worried.

'You're in for a tough time, Fenimore,' he said. 'There's all kinds of talk going around, mainly about what Cob Ogard expects to do to you. This can make you or break you. I don't like it a bit—the idea that a single roughneck like Ogard can challenge a boss like you. I told Bart Runnell as much, too.'

Luke smiled. 'And what did Runnell have to say to that?'

33

Dick flushed. 'He said you were asking for whatever you got.'

Luke chuckled. 'Just about what I'd expect him to say. I don't believe Mr. Runnell likes me very much. Which is all right with me, for that makes us even. Now don't you go to worrying, because I'm not.'

The bunkhouses and cook shacks for the construction gangs stood at the edge of town by the railroad tracks. There was one building about which a number of men were lounging, plainly waiting. Most of them were men of the different railroad gangs, but among them were a number of mule skinners and corral roustabouts, too. Which made Luke wonder a bit as to why they should be interested. On second thought he put it down to the fact that rough men of all sorts would go a long way to see a good knock-down, drag-out fight. Luke caught a glimpse of two men standing at a far corner of the building and when they saw him looking that way, they drifted from sight. One of them was Bart Runnell.

That faint, cold smile continued to play about Luke's lips, but the chill in his eyes was beginning to deepen. The waiting men gave back to let Luke and his little group through and Luke felt the measuring impact of every eye in the crowd. One mule skinner laughed coarsely and said, 'There'll be nothing to it. Ogard will eat him alive.'

Johnny Megarry put a big shoulder to the

door of the building, pushed it open. Luke followed him in. The air was thick with tobacco smoke. Men lolled on bunks, some sleeping, others talking and arguing idly back and forth. Some were playing poker or other card games at tables scattered up and down the long room between the rows of bunks.

The strong odor of men and sweat and stale air was there. The moment he entered, Luke Fenimore could sense the surliness and unrest, the avid waiting. And he thought, when you knew the moods of men like these and the strong primal tides and impulses which guided so much of their lives, you could fairly smell disorganization and truculence in a construction crew.

On a bunk near the door a man was holding forth to a number of listeners. His discourse at the moment was a growling, profane denunciation of John Guthrie, General Superintendent of the Desert & Central Railroad. He broke off abruptly as Johnny Megarry and Luke came in. All up and down the big bunkhouse heads were lifted and sullen eyes stared.

Johnny Megarry raised his big, booming, honest voice. 'Boys, meet Luke Fenimore, our new Grade Super. He's taking the place of Bole Ives.'

A stir went through the place, a sort of growl lifted. The man who had been cursing John Guthrie, cursed again, spat, and then said in a voice which reached every corner of the room, 'So! This would be the one, eh? Well I for one can't see that there is enough of him to fill the boots of Bole Ives. Not near enough!'

This, Luke knew, was the challenge. His eyes chilled until they took on the hue of glacier ice. He turned on the fellow and said curtly, 'And just who are you, my bucko friend?'

'The name is Ogard—Cob Ogard. I'm the foreman of this grade gang. And—'

'You were the foreman,' cut in Luke harshly. 'But no longer. As of this minute you're through—fired! And while I'm about it I say to your face that you're a sneaking, sniveling liar—blackguarding a man like John Guthrie behind his back. You're not fit to lick John Guthrie's boots!'

Now the growl of the room became a long, sibilant sigh. And then came dead silence. Cob Ogard stared, his black eyes moiling and filming over with a reddish glint. He came to his feet, stocky, thick and powerful, with a round, bullethead on top of a pair of burly, sloping shoulders. 'There's not enough man in you to fire me—or throw the lie in my teeth,' he exploded. 'I'll make you bleed for that.'

Luke shrugged coldly. 'We'll see. For some time now I've been hiring and firing tougher buckos than you'll ever be. But I know all the signs. You won't be satisfied until I prove it—the hard way. Step outside!'

'Ha!' barked Ogard. 'Ha! I'll break you in half!'

'You'll never do it with your dirty mouth,' said Luke. 'Step outside!'

Johnny Megarry was still worried. As Luke led the way out, Johnny touched his arm. 'He's a bad one, Luke. Never let him get hold of you, for anything goes with Ogard. He'll gouge and butt and stamp. He'll wreck you for life if he can. He'll put the boots to you if he can get you down. It's what he'll try to do.'

Luke shrugged. 'Like I said at breakfast, I've met his kind before. They're tough if you fight them their way, but not near so tough if you don't. But he may have some friends lined up to buy in if things start going against him. You'll watch for that?'

'I'll watch, and I'll break the back of any man who tries it,' Johnny vowed.

The word had spread with mysterious speed. Every bunkhouse emptied to the last man and others came hurrying in from all directions. They crowded around, avid as wolves. Now Luke saw Bart Runnell again and with him was a lurching, shifty-eyed individual with a big, loose mouth and the heavy flush of too much whisky on his mottled face. That, thought Luke, would be Bole Ives.

Luke took off his hat and his fleece-lined coat. The chill air laid a swift bite across his shoulders. He tossed the hat and coat to Joe Keller, saying easily, 'Hold these for a minute or two, Joe.'

Luke tightened the belt about his lean, hard-packed waist another notch, flexed his arms and shoulders and turned to face Ogard. No longer was Luke a quiet, faintly smiling man with a certain aloof remoteness about him. Now, as he moved forward, he was a soft-stepping, prowling panther, committed to a cold, remorseless purpose.

Cob Ogard stood with feet spread, thick legs bent in a slight crouch. He held his hands half before him, elbows bent, fingers splayed, ready to grab and rend and tear. His lips were parted in a tight snarl. He looked like an ape, ready to pounce and destroy.

Luke did not wait for Ogard to move in. Instead, he slithered lightly forward, his left hand shooting out rapier-fast and straight. There was vastly more behind the punch than there seemed to be, for it snapped Ogard's bullethead back and brought a gouting burst of crimson from his mashed lips. It sent a startled gasp through the watching crowd and it set Cob Ogard berserk, as it was calculated to do. Ogard leaped, fingers spread and clawing, hoping to get in close where he could get a grip and wrestle his man down.

But Luke was already away. Side-stepping, as Ogard lunged past, Luke brought his right fist across with a hard, slashing roll of his shoulders behind the blow. This time his target was the side of Ogard's bull neck, close up

38

under the ear, and Luke's ridged knuckles found the nerve there fairly. Ogard went sprawling, numbed and shaken.

Now indeed did a long sigh go over the crowd, as though it had just witnessed something no man thought possible. Cob Ogard was down, knocked off his feet by a single, driving punch.

At the inner rim of the watchers, Casey O'Keefe hugged himself. 'He knows how,' Casey chortled, with no one listening to him. 'The lad knows how. He can hit and he can get away. This day does Cob Ogard get his full needings!'

Cob Ogard got up slowly, shaking his head as though completely bewildered at what had happened to him. He glared red-eyed at Luke, a fan of crimson dribbling down from his pouting lips. 'Come to me!' he bawled. 'Come to me like a man. I'll tear your head off!'

'Come and get me!' taunted Luke. 'I thought you were a real bucko boy, as tough as they're made. Why, I've seen old men with whiskers who could handle the likes of you. Come and get me!'

Ogard took the bait. Again he charged in and again he took that wicked, jarring left to the face, twice without showing any ability at defense at all. Which was all Luke wanted to find out. Here was a typical rough-and-tumble fighter, a mauler, a gouger, one to knee, to choke and batter and use every dirty trick in

39

the book—if he could get close enough.

Luke flailed that wicked left again and opened a cut under Ogard's eye.

Bole Ives it was who had been with Bart Runnell. His first confidence in Cob Ogard's ability was fast vanishing. Ogard was battered and bleeding and had been down once, while the lean, icy-eyed man facing him was untouched, unmarked, cool and deadly. So now Ives came pushing through to the center of the circle, big and gross and loosemouthed. He let out a string of curses.

'Get him, Cob—get him! Kick his ribs in. I want a swing at him myself!'

If Bole Ives hoped by this means to start others in the crowd after Luke Fenimore, he was quickly disillusioned, for, as he took another step forward Johnny Megarry's huge paw closed on his shoulder and Ives was whirled violently back and aside. 'No you don't, Ives! None of that!' rumbled Johnny. 'This is a fair fight between the two of them, and it's of Ogard's brag and asking. You'll not be mixing in—you or any other. Don't argue with me or I'll twist your good-for-nothin' drunken neck. Back away!'

Bole Ives backed, cursing.

That slashing left hand which seemed always in his face maddened Cob Ogard completely. Yet, there was an animal cunning in him and he tried a treacherous ruse. He lunged forward, whirled and kicked, slashing his booted foot in from the side, trying to cut Luke's feet from under him. But Luke had seen this kind of trick tried before and, instead of trying to dodge it, he moved in close, his waiting right ripping across. It crashed home and with Ogard on one foot and off balance, the blow seemed to turn him half over in the air. So Ogard was down again.

Cob Ogard now lost all power of self-control. He came up, bawling and yelling like a mad animal, blind and crazy with his own frustrated rage. He came in wildly, clumsily, wide open, and Luke hit him twice, first with that rush-stopping left and then with a whistling right cross, with everything Luke possessed behind the blow. It landed squarely where he aimed it, on the point of Ogard's jaw. This time Ogard fell forward, landing on his hands and knees, where he stayed for a moment, bullethead rolling from side to side.

He got up slowly, dazed and badly hurt. And now Luke went after him savagely. This wasn't just a lesson to Cob Ogard. This was a lesson for every man in the gang. It was part of a psychology which Luke Fenimore had learned long ago, back along the rough, tough years of his apprenticeship in the ways of construction crews and of the men who made up such crews. This was a lesson in who was boss.

Luke gave Ogard no chance to find either physical or mental balance again. His fists,

41

rock-hard and merciless, winged in like projectiles from a gun. They drove Cob Ogard back and back, slowly at first, then faster and faster as the cumulative punishment they handed out built up to a point where Ogard's physical resistance would no longer absorb it. So then, presently, Ogard was down once more, flat on his face this time—and he did not get up. The fight was over. It had not lasted long, it had been definitely one-sided. And now it was finished.

For a moment Luke Fenimore stood, watching his man, taut and tight-strung for further combat, if it were needed. When he saw definitely that it was not, his shoulders loosened and relaxed and he turned, his glance running over the stunned and silent crowd. A tight smile edged his lips again, hard but not unfriendly.

'Well,' he said, 'this was what you wanted to see, wasn't it? A fight? All right, you've seen it and now it's over and done with. But I'm moving into another fight, a real, worth-while one this time, and I want you men in it with me. We've got a railroad to build. Forty-five miles of it and with just thirty-four days left to do it in. There'll be some who will say it can't be done. They'll be wrong. It can be done and we're going to prove it. We're going out and move dirt like it was never moved before. The train is waiting to take us out to the job. Let's get down to it!'

He turned away, took his hat and coat from Joe Keller, donned them, his back to the crowd. He seemed to be utterly sure of these men, but he wasn't. Though he showed no outward sign of the fact, deep down inside him Luke was fairly holding his breath. For this was the big test. If they followed him now, then he had them. They would never let him down, never doubt him. He knew men like these, knew that once they cast their full allegiance, they would never call it back.

He knew their simple, fundamental creeds. Their work was physical, so it was only natural that their judgment of a man should be mainly by a physical yardstick. Courage they would rate first of all. Then strength, ability, physical toughness. It was in them to love a fighter and a leader. Luke was wondering if he had offered them both of these.

He started for the tracks, where the Simcoe engine and the little string of cars waited. Joe Keller dropped in on one side of him, Johnny Megarry on the other. And then from behind a voice yelled, 'Okay, boss! Comin' right with you!'

That did it. Luke heard the clatter of boots, sensed the surge of bodies. Before he reached the cars, men were pushing ahead, laughing and talking excitedly as they clambered up onto the flats. Something swelled up inside of Luke, caught him by the throat. This, he thought, could be a big moment in a man's life.

As Alec Craigie and Casey O'Keefe climbed into the cab of the Simcoe, Alec said, 'I heard John Guthrie tell Joe Keller that he was going to bring in a trouble shooter to clean things up in the grade gang. Guthrie sure didn't make any mistake.'

Casey reached for the whistle cord, sent two sharp toots echoing. Then he leaned from his window and yelled, 'Shake it up, you terriers— shake it up! We got a job to do!'

There was a last-minute rush. The little narrow-gauge flatcars were jammed with men and their tools. Casey looked across the cab and said, 'Roll her, Alec—they're all aboard. Man! What a broth of a lad Luke Fenimore is with his maulies!'

The end of grade was not over two hundred yards ahead of the end of steel. But it was obvious now that the grade crew intended to do something about this in a hurry. With Johnny Megarry showing the way the men went at things almost on the run. Picks began to thud, shovels to scrape and clang. Mules brought from a temporary corral close by were harnessed and hitched to Fresno scrapers in record time. It was almost as though these men were ashamed of their past unruliness and wanted to make good for it.

Joe Keller stood beside Luke Fenimore, watching. 'That,' he said gravely, 'is the best display of spirit I've seen on this job yet. It would seem that you've licked your trouble

44

quick, Luke, while mine is just beginning to get real tough. See that flat of steel we brought out with us? Well, that's the last of it.'

'I heard that the steel angle was bad,' Luke nodded. 'And Bart Runnell muffed out on that secondhand steel he was sent after. Joe, there are a few angles about this layout I can't exactly figure.'

Joe Keller flashed Luke a quick look. 'You're not the only one who is fighting his head, about this and that. Well, getting the steel is the job of somebody a lot higher up than me. All I can do is lay it. And I'll do that, just as fast as they get it to me and grade is laid down to take it. I'm just a gang boss. There are limits to what I can do.'

Joe went back to supervise the unloading of the flat of steel. Dick Leslie came over beside Luke. There was something almost like awe and hero worship in the boyish engineer's manner. Luke understood, and grinned. 'I'm not that good, Dick. Ogard didn't have a thing, really.'

Dick shrugged. 'All I know is that until you came along, Cob Ogard was the bucko boy of this railroad. So I'm thinking it and I might as well say it. You're a whole damned lot of man, Luke.'

Luke chuckled. 'I'm glad you think so, Dick; that will give me a lift in my weaker moments. And now, what do you think of Johnny Megarry to take Ogard's place as foreman of the grade gang?'

'Perfect,' answered Dick simply. 'The men like him and he's a horse for work. And you can depend on him with your life.'

'My own judgment,' nodded Luke. 'So it'll be that way. I'll go tell him.'

Johnny Megarry took the news very solemnly. 'If you think I'm the man for the job, Luke, I'll give you my best. I'm hoping the boys will approve.'

'We'll see,' said Luke. 'Come along.'

The men did approve. Luke gave out the word casually as he moved here and there through the gang and it met with nods of approval all along the line. One of the Fresno-scraper men grinned and said, 'If the big fellow has got half in his head what he has in his back, he'll be movin' mountains for you, Mr. Fenimore.'

The rest of the day was a very busy one for Luke. He was on the move constantly, concentrating on getting the gang molded into a smooth working unit. Up and down he tramped, Johnny Megarry at his side. He gave orders here, dropped suggestions there, studying his men and their capabilities, placing them in the spots where they could really turn in their best work. But there was always the spice of humor in Luke's eyes and a smile on his lips which leavened the weight of his authority.

It went over with the men. They saw that he

46

knew his business, that he was fair, that he knew how to spot the weak links in the chain and correct them. He knew how to organize against waste motion. And he wasn't afraid to get his hands dirty. Several times he lent his weight to the dump handle of a heavily loaded scraper. He moved among the pick-and-shovel men and he spoke their language, too. He grabbed a crowbar and sweated right along with the men for a full quarter of an hour as they toiled to dislodge a huge, stubborn boulder and roll it out of the way. The sum total of it all was that dirt moved and moved fast and the raw scar of the new grade grew and lengthened by the hour.

Behind the immediate details of his own job, Luke was thinking about steel. It was as he had told Dick Leslie. You couldn't build a railroad without steel. Steel was the payoff, the one thing there was no possible substitute for. You could, in a pinch, lay steel across almost any kind of terrain—if you had it. But you had to have it. Steel!

It was, as a man thought about it, almost incredible that any road building against a time limit, and with a big and vitally needed subsidy as the goal, would allow itself to be caught short on steel. It all added up to a lot of things without any right answers, and Luke made up his mind to get some of those answers at the first opportunity.

The wagon road between Castle Mountain

and Cold Creek traveled the valley of the Castle River also, and about midafternoon a full dozen big freight outfits, heavy and groaning under their loads of lead pigs, came rolling slowly along, drawn by long strings of toiling, sweating mules. Skinners humped stoically on the corner box of the wagons, jerklines across their knees, long-lashed whips looped in their hands. On one of the outfits, two men rode the box and this wagon pulled to the side of the road and stopped opposite Luke's hard-rustling gang. One of the men climbed down off the wagon and came over.

He was tall and lank, with a heavily boned face and shrewd, squinty eyes. He said to Johnny Megarry, 'Plenty of industry today, eh? Where's Bole Ives and Cob Ogard?'

'Through,' answered Johnny bluntly.

The newcomer blinked. 'That's news. Who's replacing them?'

'Luke Fenimore yonder is in charge. I'm the new foreman.'

The newcomer gave Luke a narrow-eyed, steady regard. 'Must be a good man. Never saw this crew put out like it is now.'

'He is a good man,' Johnny said. 'He gave Cob Ogard the beating of his life and never even raised a sweat. Maybe you'd like to meet him?'

'I would that.'

Johnny led the way over to Luke and said, 'Shake hands with Jack Fargo, Luke. You've

48

heard of Jack. He handles all the freight between Cold Creek and Castle Mountain.'

Fargo shook hands heartily. 'Glad to know you, Fenimore. You sure got this gang digging in. What did you do, give 'em a shot of hop? If you did,' he added with a grin, 'how's to borrow some of the stuff? I got a lot of jiggers drawing wages from me who could stand some of the same.'

Luke smiled briefly, that guarded remoteness deepening in his eyes. It was as though he was erecting a wall against Fargo's effusiveness. 'They're a good gang,' he said. 'All they needed was a chance to go. Ah— Fargo, I believe I met three of your men coming in from Garnet, yesterday.'

Fargo's smile went a trifle set. 'No men of mine over that way. My business all runs from Cold Creek south.'

'These three,' went on Luke, 'got on the train at Kicking Horse water tower. For some reason they didn't want me to come on through to Cold Creek. They felt pretty strongly about it, so strongly they were willing to argue the point. It was pretty rough for a couple of minutes, but they couldn't quite make their point. Instead of me getting off, they did. Thought you might be interested to hear about it.'

'You're talking riddles as far as I'm concerned,' declared Fargo. 'I can't think of any reason why men of mine should pull such a

49

fool stunt. Somebody is mistaken, somewhere. Who said they were my men?'

'The brakie on the train said he'd seen at least one of them skinning an outfit for you at one time.'

Fargo shrugged. 'That could be,' he admitted. 'Like everybody else in the freighting game, I hire 'em and I fire 'em. Mule skinners come and go. So, for the Lord's sake, don't hold me responsible for some dumb play pulled by some no-account skinner who might have worked for me at one time. That doesn't make sense.'

Luke smiled again. 'That could have been the way it happened, sure enough.'

Jack Fargo hung around for some little time, talking of this and that, his shrewd eyes not missing a trick. Then, with a careless wave of his hand he went back to his wagon and the big freight outfit resumed its toiling, creaking way. Luke turned to Johnny Megarry.

'Fargo stands to lose quite a chunk of freighting business, once we put steel to Castle Mountain. Ever think of that, Johnny?'

Johnny nodded. 'That he does. But it's the story of the West, Luke, when the steel comes in the freighters quit rolling. It was the freighters that put the pack trains out of business, and the pack trains that took the loads off the backs of men. Things change. It's the way of the world.'

'A shrewd man, Fargo,' murmured Luke.

'And a profit-hungry one, by the look of him.'

Johnny boomed a chuckle. 'You've a shrewd eye yourself for reading a man. And now, what was this talk about a ruckus of some sort while you were coming in past Kicking Horse?'

'Just three rough ones who needed a lesson in manners. It wasn't much,' Luke said carelessly.

Yet he stared after the departing freight outfit with a speculative gravity.

When Alec Craigie and Casey O'Keefe came rolling out in the Simcoe engine, pushing a little string of flats ahead of them through the fading afternoon sunshine, it was a tired but contented gang of men who climbed onto the flats for the trip back to Cold Creek. Luke, watching the men, saw several of them look back at the stretch of new grade they had opened up and marked the satisfaction in their eyes. He heard one of the men say to another, 'Those steel-laying monkeys have been hollerin' for more grade to work on. From here on out we'll throw new grade at them until we break their hearts.'

To Johnny Megarry, as they found places on the tail car, Luke said, 'Men are only truly happy when they've accomplished something. Work, and the products of work, are what men find pride in. The day is coming when we're going to be mighty proud of this gang of ours, Johnny.'

They were walking up the street of Cold

51

Creek toward Ma Megarry's boarding house when Luke realized that Bart Runnell hadn't shown up on the job all day, and he remarked on this. Johnny Megarry nodded and said, 'I had thought of that myself. But it may be that John Guthrie called him somewhere else.'

They were at the supper table when Ma Megarry, coming in with a huge platter of food, said, 'John Guthrie is back in town, Mr. Fenimore. And he sent word that he wants to see you at his room in the hotel this evening.'

'Thanks, Ma,' nodded Luke. 'Now I've a word for you. What do you think of your Johnny? He's the new foreman of the gang.'

Ma's face lighted up like a sunbeam. 'Is he now?' she exclaimed pridefully. 'Well, it is high time that the worth of him was being rightfully recognized.'

Big Johnny flushed painfully. 'I'm not so sure of that. There are times when this head of mine can be awful thick.'

'Bosh!' said Ma, giving him an affectionate buffet. 'It's only your modesty speakin', John Megarry. You're the equal of any man who ever walked.'

'My exact opinion, Ma,' applauded Luke.

Ma eyed Luke musingly. 'From all I hear, you're quite a broth of a man yourself, Luke Fenimore. It's said that this morning you gave that Cob Ogard a fearful whipping. And there are some who liked the fact and some who did not.'

'For instance?'

'Well,' said Ma slowly, 'I saw Bart Runnell coming back up the street and, sure, he looked like he had just finished swallowing a pint of vinegar. And this evenin', just before you boys came in, there was that nice lad, Dick Leslie, takin' his sister home, her with a market basket on her arm. Dick was telling her all about it and fair shoutin' with glee.'

'The young cub shouldn't have done that,' growled Luke. 'No sense telling a nice girl like Miss Leslie about a rough, knock-down and drag-out brawl. A thing of that sort would only disgust her.'

Ma Megarry smiled very wisely. 'It's plain, Luke Fenimore, that there is much you do not understand about women. While it's true no good woman likes brutality, at the same time never did any good woman look too sideways at a man willing and able to uphold the right of things with his fists.'

Luke got off the subject quickly. 'Did John Guthrie send any word of what he wanted?'

'Only that you go see him, Luke.'

Half an hour later, Luke knocked at Guthrie's door and found the General Superintendent alone. John Guthrie was a man of medium size, his hair and crisp mustache grizzled with middle age. He looked tired and harassed and he grasped Luke's hand almost eagerly.

'Come in, man—come in,' he exclaimed.

53

'I've been anxious to know how you found things and what you think of our chances of getting in under the deadline now that you've had opportunity to look things over. Have a chair—have a cigar!'

Luke did both, and got the cigar to drawing smoothly before speaking. Then he said slowly, 'I'm glad of this chance to talk to you, Mr. Guthrie. For, though I've only been around little more than a day I've run across some angles I simply can't understand and which make it appear to me that we'll need nothing short of a miracle or two to get us into Castle Mountain ahead of that subsidy deadline. For instance how in the name of all that makes common sense did this outfit allow itself to be caught short on steel? Steel—of all things!'

Guthrie rolled his cigar back and forth in his lips. Abruptly he waved a hand in hard decision. 'I'm through pulling punches to keep somebody else from being bruised, and then have all the blame heaped on me. Primarily, we are short of steel because of Henry Shard.'

Luke's head jerked up. 'Henry Shard! Why, as I understand it, he is one of the three men most interested in getting this road built; one of the three owners of it.'

'That's right, he is,' said Guthrie dryly. 'Three men, Shard, Frank Ames and Curtis Leffingwell. They hold the purse strings. Henry Shard is the treasurer. He is what some people might call a good businessman. He expects, and demands, a full dollar of value for every dollar spent. I've heard it said that he wants even a dollar and five cents of value for every dollar he spends. Be that as it may, the fact remains that Shard tried to shop around among the mills in the East for steel. He tried to bargain.'

'There's a place to pinch pennies,' said Luke, 'and a place not to. You can't build a road without steel. What the hell!'

'Exactly!' Guthrie nodded. 'To begin with, as railroads go, we are just a little narrow-gauge, jerkline, wildcat outfit. When we are all done, we'll be just ninety miles long. Given time, the mills will get the steel to us, but it isn't reasonable to expect them to drop an order for hundreds of miles of standard-gauge hundred-pound steel for some big job just to get our dinky little order out in a hurry. Even so, we'd have had our steel if Shard had placed the full order to begin with. I tried to get him to do it, but he refused. He said it would tie up too much money at one time, which might be needed for other expenses. So he has been buying ten or fifteen miles of steel at a time. Which would be quite all right and maybe good, sound financing—if we had plenty of time ahead of us. But on a deal like this it can be suicide. Now there's no telling when the next shipment of steel will be along. That Henry Shard! He can be the most self-opinionated, ultra-conservative, pigheaded old buzzard!'

'It would seem that there isn't a lick of sense in me beating my head off at building grade if there isn't going to be any steel to lay on it,' growled Luke. 'What about this secondhand steel Runnell was supposed to round up?'

'That was from the Grasshopper silver strike that looked like it might be a second Comstock lode—but wasn't. In the first flush of the boom a narrow-gauge road was started. Some fifteen or twenty miles of road had been built when the boom went bust. Runnell was sent out to get that steel. We were late. Another outfit had beat us to it.' Here a despondent weariness settled over Guthrie like a heavy cloak. 'I was depending a great deal on getting hold of that steel.'

Luke stirred restlessly. 'I don't know why I should really give a thin damn one way or the other. I got nothing at stake here. But I never tied into a job yet that I ran out on. And I like to see a job get done. That Grasshopper fiasco wasn't the only boom town in Nevada that went bust. There were plenty of camps—'

He broke off, staring at the far wall through a haze of cigar smoke. A gleam came into his eyes. 'I know a man with more railroad savvy than any other I ever met. A man who might know—' Luke broke off again, jumping to his feet. 'Care to give me authority to see that man, Mr. Guthrie?'

'If,' said John Guthrie grimly, 'there's a chance to round up some steel, I'll give you authority to see the King of Siam. Who is this man, Luke?'

'Warren Garland.'

'Warren Garland! Why he's the Division Superintendent of the transcontinental at LeMoyne. He's much too big a man to bother his head with such as us.'

'I never found him too big to lend an ear—and a friendly one—to anything that has to do with railroad construction,' Luke declared. 'And if there is any narrow-gauge steel lying around loose, he's the one man most likely to know about it. There's an Overland through Garnet at eight-ten tomorrow morning that I can catch if I can get to Garnet in time.'

'I'll see that Alec Craigie and Casey O'Keefe get you there, Luke. I'd even run you to Garnet in the Simcoe myself if it will get us a few more miles of steel. Anything—just so we can make progress. But how about your gang?'

Luke said, 'Johnny Megarry can handle it. A good boy, Johnny. We'll keep this under our hats, Mr. Guthrie, until we know the yes or no of it. Because I've bumped into one or two angles that don't add up—don't add up at all.'

Meeting Luke's look, John Guthrie nodded slowly. 'And I, Luke, I'm glad to know that someone else has found cause to wonder about this and that, and that it hasn't been a

57

product of my own imagination. Er—you believe, then, that there is more to some of our troubles than meets the casual eye?'

'I'd bet hard money on it, Mr. Guthrie. From all I hear and see, too many things have gone wrong all at once to be just a matter of mere coincidence. Well, I'll be rolling in the morning.'

'I'll see that Alec Craigie and Casey O'Keefe are notified and will be all ready for the run,' promised Guthrie. 'And while it is all a thin gamble, I think I'll sleep a little better for it, tonight.'

Puffing thoughtfully on his cigar, Luke headed back for the boardinghouse. On his way he passed the Big Sage saloon. He glanced casually in through a window, stopped short and took a look. A little group of three men stood at the bar. One of them was Cob Ogard, face blackened and bruised and swollen from the weight of Luke's fists. Another was Bole Ives, big and gross. The third was lanky, rawboned Jack Fargo, the freighter boss. A glass of whisky stood in front of each of the three, but they seemed to have far more on their minds than just a drink of whisky. Their heads were together, with Jack Fargo talking emphatically. The others took much interest in what Fargo was saying.

Luke went on and presently glanced across the night to where the Leslie cabin stood, warm light glowing in its windows. He thought

58

of that light gleaming on a girl's dark head, and laying tender shadows about her lips and chin and throat. Then he shook himself, half angrily.

'Quit it, Fenimore, you damned fool!' he muttered. 'You saw once how Bart Runnell fills her eye. She never could have any use for a construction-camp roughneck like you. All you can hope for is that when some of these queer tangles begin to unwind, they won't show anything that might hurt her too bad. For she's too fine to be hurt.'

At Ma Megarry's Luke found Johnny Megarry doing a bit of fixing on the big cooking range in Ma's kitchen. He drew Johnny aside and said, 'You'll be running the job alone for a while, Johnny. The gang is straightened out pretty well now and you shouldn't have any trouble. If anyone asks where I am, tell them I've been called away for a few days, but that I'll be back. Can do, big feller?'

Johnny nodded, 'Can do, Luke.'

CHAPTER THREE

STEEL BUCCANEER

Warren Garland was a spare, loosely knit man with a bear-trap jaw and keen but humorous eyes. He sat loose and relaxed in his office at LeMoyne and listened intently to Luke Fenimore's story.

'So there it is, Mr. Garland,' ended Luke. 'I've tied in with an outfit that is trying to build a narrow-gauge railroad without sure delivery of steel. Strictly speaking, steel is none of my affair. I was hired to run grade and I know I can put the grade through to Castle Mountain ahead of that subsidy deadline. Yet, there's a challenge in this thing that intrigues me and there are several good men in the setup to whom the successful completion of the job means a great deal. I'd like to see them put it over, and have a hand in it myself. But we've got to have steel, so I'm out after it. We missed out on getting that Grasshopper steel, but I thought you might know of a similar case of some secondhand narrow-gauge steel we might pick up.'

Warren Garland grinned. 'Now that you mention it, Luke, there might be something out at Corinth that could interest you.' Garland glanced at his watch, reached for his hat. 'There's a local freight through in exactly four minutes. We'll ride it as far as Corinth.'

'No need of you going out to Corinth, Mr. Garland,' protested Luke. 'You're too busy a man to bother—'

Warren Garland clapped Luke on the shoulder, pushed him out of the office door. 'Busy? Listen, Luke—I'm tickled pink for you bringing me an excuse to get out of this damned office for a while. I'm not busy. I'm just bored stiff. All I do is sit around on my fanny and look wise while the staff does all the work. I had a lot more fun in the old days when I really had jobs to do. Now I've just become a damn figurehead—looking wise and getting dumber by the minute. I envy you your job. Come on.'

So the two of them rode the freight caboose as far as Corinth, which was little more than a wire stop and an east-west siding for emergencies.

A hundred yards to the east, on the north side of the main line, were a couple of dilapidated, tumble-down sheds, the largest of which still carried smoke and soot stains. Sagebrush grew right up to the sides of the sheds. As he led the way over to the ramshackle structures, Warren Garland indicated a ragged, uneven break in the brush, running away to the north.

'There, Luke,' he said, 'is about all that remains of another of mankind's dizzy dreams.

Some thirty miles north of here a silver lead was opened up. There was a rush and the usual talk of another bonanza. A narrow-gauge railroad started to build, and got about a dozen miles along, when the silver lead ran out and the rainbow collapsed. Almost identical to that Grasshopper fiasco. You know, it really was too bad that your people couldn't have beaten Western Mining Syndicate and that fellow Fargo to the Grasshopper steel, for it was a later project than this by several years. And—'

'Wait a minute,' broke in Luke. 'Did you say—Fargo?'

'Why, yes. I'm sure that was the name. I remembered it particularly because it was a trifle unusual. I got the story about fourth-hand, just gossip along the line. And as I got it, this Western Mining Syndicate is some newly formed outfit. I suppose we'll hear more of them one of these days. They may be going to try and open up that Grasshopper camp again—either that or promote another narrow-gauge out to some prospector's pipe dream of a thriving and permanent camp. The old, old song. Ring in the suckers, rake in the dough.'

Luke said nothing more, but far back in his eyes a cold, grim gleam was dancing. It was as though he was beginning to find answers to several things.

Warren Garland tramped open a clump of

sage. 'Here's your steel, Luke. Plenty of rust, but still steel, inside. And by the way, your people couldn't use another locomotive, could they? Come take a look.'

He led the way into the smoke-stained shed. Sure enough, there it stood, festooned with cobwebs, dirt and debris and smeared with rust. Yet, it was a narrow-gauge locomotive. Warren Garland reached up and scrubbed a palm across the manufacturer's name plate.

'Union Foundry,' he grunted. 'Huh! That *is* an old-timer.' He grinned. 'Still, it seems to have wheels. Chances are, with a few days of work by somebody who knows how, plus some oil and grease in the right places, you might get a wheeze or two out of her yet. In my time I've seen worse. If you're interested in this bucket of rust, Luke, I'll loan you a couple of good men from the round house at Lemoyne, and let them see what they can do toward putting it in shape. Which reminds me. There's a siding yonder with a couple of old flats on it. The sage has grown up around 'em till they're nearly covered.'

The siding and the flats were there all right. Rickety the flatcars were, their ironwork brown with rust. But, like the old engine, they had wheels and would roll. 'You can use 'em to haul the steel out as you tear it up,' Garland suggested.

'I can hardly believe it,' said Luke. 'Like something straight from heaven. Who, I

63

wonder, owns the layout?'

'Lord! I wouldn't know,' answered Garland. 'I wouldn't have known it was here if a minor wreck hadn't brought me out here about six months ago. I got curious about what these sheds might hold, so I wandered over for a look. After that I was interested enough to run down some of the background of the affair. But as to who really owns this junk, I've no idea. Whoever does own it apparently didn't consider it worth salvaging. But you should worry. You need steel—must have it, from what you've been saying. Here it is. Take it and worry about the rest later. Your people can always pay for it, once they locate the owner. If you should run into any trouble over it, come and see me. I can generally wangle an angle or two that'll help.'

'You,' said Luke, 'are the whitest white man I know.'

'Pshaw!' scoffed Garland. 'This is fun. I really envy you, Luke. Plenty of times I look back longingly to the days when it was a triumph every time we got a train through. Now things run so smoothly I feel like a useless appendage. As I told you, all I do is sit around and look wise. Besides, I like to see these little feeder lines, such as you folks are building, prosper, providing they are sound and legitimate. Those Castle Mountain mines are sound and proven; and it's good business for us to see you make the grade.'

Luke stretched his arms wide, impatient for action. 'If I had wings,' he said, 'I'd break all records from here to Cold Creek.'

Warren Garland looked at his watch and grinned again. 'Seeing that you haven't, we'll have to depend on wheels and steam. We'll catch Twenty-eight back to LeMoyne in half an hour.'

*   *   *

When Luke Fenimore got off a westbound main liner at Garnet, it was to see the little Simcoe, headlight shining in the early dusk, come rolling up from the south with half a dozen lead-laden flats. Luke went over and climbed up into the cab.

'Hello, Fenimore,' said Alec Craigie. 'Mr. Guthrie said for us to keep a lookout for you. He said you might have a message to send along to him.'

'I want to deliver the message myself, boys,' said Luke. 'It's important enough to be delivered tonight, if possible.'

Craigie turned to his fireman. 'How about it, Casey?'

'Hell, yes!' growled Casey O'Keefe. 'If it's anything that'll get things movin' with this damned outfit.'

"It is,' said Luke. 'It's steel.'

'Ha!' exclaimed Alec Craigie. 'That does listen good. Soon as we shunt these flats to the

65

siding we'll head for Cold Creek.'

Free of all load, deadheading back, the Simcoe really rolled. Once, above the clatter and clank, Alec Craigie said, 'John Guthrie needs something to cheer him up. Because the Castle Mountain crowd are at Cold Creek and from all I heard they really had the Old Man on the spot.'

The miles clicked away. They topped out over Rockaway Pass and fled down toward the valley of the Castle River beyond. Alec Craigie sent the long bay of his whistle out to greet the lights of Cold Creek. Luke was swinging from the cab even before the Simcoe rolled to a stop. 'Thanks a lot, boys,' he called. 'I won't forget this favor.'

Luke hurried straight to the hotel and to John Guthrie's room. The door was locked. Behind it sounded the growl of voices, angry voices. Luke knocked solidly and it was John Guthrie who opened the door. He looked harassed and weary and angry. At the sight of Luke his face lighted up.

'Luke! You wouldn't be back so soon if you didn't have good news. Come in, man—come in!'

Bart Runnell was there, looking sulky. And three other men whom Luke had never seen before. John Guthrie said, 'This is Luke Fenimore, gentlemen—the man I've been telling you about. Luke, shake hands with Frank Ames, Curt Leffingwell and Henry

Shard.'

Shard was a thin, round-shouldered man, with a narrow face, a tight mouth and a long, pointed nose. Leffingwell was broad and burly, blunt-featured, with a certain masklike inscrutability. Frank Ames was a rosy, roly-poly little man with a wide and humorous mouth. His eyes were brisk and alert, showing keen intelligence.

The room was heavy with argument and strain and tobacco smoke. 'We've been,' said John Guthrie a trifle awkwardly, 'discussing our troubles, Luke. Among others, that lack of steel.'

'I've located some steel, John. Twelve miles of it.'

'Ah!' said Curt Leffingwell. 'And it can be had?'

'It can be had. Also a locomotive, an old Union Foundry job. Not in the best of shape, but I think it can be made to earn its keep. Then there are a couple of flats. The same.'

Frank Ames said, 'That's the best news I've heard in a month of Sundays. Go on, Fenimore—go on! Where—and how?'

Luke told them, describing the layout at Corinth. 'Warren Garland said he'd put some of his best mechanics to work on the engine and get it in running shape for us. With that to pull the two old flats, we can strip the steel off that old road in a hurry. It's all there if you want it, gentlemen.'

'If we want it!' breathed John Guthrie.

Henry Shard cleared his throat. 'There is,' he said in thin harshness, 'a question or two to be answered. Who owns that steel and rolling stock, Fenimore—and what will be the price?'

'That I don't know,' answered Luke. 'Neither does Warren Garland. It is Mr. Garland's opinion that whoever does own it has abandoned it as not being worth the price of salvage. He suggests, and I agree with him, that we take it now and deal with the owners later, when and if we can locate them.'

Shard gave a short, barking, sarcastic laugh. 'Young man, you have plenty of enthusiasm but not much business sense. This railroad of ours is a practical business investment, not a gambling institution. We've no desire to be faced with a ruinous lawsuit. We'll be glad to get that Corinth steel, yes—when we have located the owners, negotiated a fair price and closed the deal. But until that time we do not touch it. That's final!'

Luke had been on the go. He had burned up a lot of nervous energy over this thing. He hadn't eaten in better than twelve hours. He had been buoyed high with enthusiasm over the prospects of what he had found and what it could mean. Now, with one harsh, almost sneering remark, Henry Shard had put a crusher on the whole thing.

Luke looked around. Bart Runnell had a faint smirk on his face, but Frank Ames and

Curt Leffingwell were watching with unreadable eyes. Luke's own eyes began to smoke up as bitter anger rose in him.

'All right,' he said, his voice going bleak. 'All right! To hell with all of you but John Guthrie. I thought you had a railroad to build against a deadline to get a state subsidy. I thought this was a job for men with guts and punch. I was wrong. It's a layout of penny-pinching fools. You seem to be playing with the jackass idea that you can build a railroad without steel, that you can beat a deadline by shopping for prices and bargaining for a few nickels. You hire a good man in John Guthrie and expect him to get results—yet all the time you tie his hands by not furnishing him with enough material and equipment to do the job. Hell! It's a joke! I don't know why I should give a damn, but I did, plenty—up to now. But no more!'

Luke spun to face John Guthrie. 'I'm sorry, John—but this is it. You better let Runnell hire back Bole Ives and Cob Ogard. They seem to be the kind of faithful little busy bees these people want. As for me, I'm leaving in the morning.'

'I think,' said John Guthrie quietly, 'that you've got something there, Luke. I'll be leaving with you.' He turned to face the others. 'When I took this job I knew it was going to be a tough one, with every day and every mile counting strongly. I told you that. I told you we couldn't afford any mistakes, any delays. I had

69

your promise that there'd be none of either and it was a promise that hasn't been kept. My reputation is pretty fair, and, such as it is, I don't intend to throw it away by beating my head against a wall of penuriousness and short-sighted caution. You have my resignation, gentlemen—effective immediately!'

'No!' It was Curt Leffingwell who spoke, and there was a growl in his voice. 'Neither you nor Fenimore is leaving, John. Shard hasn't the whole say in this deal—not by a hell of a lot. Frank Ames and I have just as much at stake as he has. And if I know Frank Ames—and I think I do—I'm sure I speak for him as well as for myself when I say— Fenimore, you go get that steel, that engine and those flatcars!'

Henry Shard stirred. 'I won't be party to such a deal,' he shrilled. 'I refuse to accept any such—'

Leffingwell swung around, his heavy jaw thrusting out. 'Shut up, Henry! I'm having my say and while I'm at it, let's call a spade a spade. We've been three damn fools, you and Frank and I. We let you handle the purchasing end of things because we knew how far you could make a dollar go, and, frankly, that was all right. Because there is a limit to our capital. However, you've been so damned tight and full of penny-ante tactics over prices with the mills we're now left hanging in the air for steel. Well, we're through with that sort of business.

70

We're going after that Corinth steel, taking it, and settling for it later in whatever manner we have to.'

Leffingwell turned to Runnell, and his voice had a bite to it. 'Runnell, you're on damned thin ice. You botched the Grasshopper steel job and didn't seem too put out over the failure. Before that you let the grade gang get out of hand and didn't seem a damn bit interested in doing anything about that. I'm beginning to wonder just how much you really know about railroading and just why we're paying you a salary. Fenimore here has made you look silly. He's plenty big enough man to handle your job, and he'll have it, unless you come to life and begin pulling your share of the load. Now you know! Frank, is there anything you want to add?'

Frank Ames chuckled. 'Not a thing, Curt—except amen. I think you've cleared the air considerably. Which it needed.' He turned to Guthrie. 'John, it seems we haven't done our best by you up to now, but I promise you a complete change in the future. You and Fenimore go ahead and build this road for us. Build it and beat that deadline. Use whatever means you have to, to get it done, and know you have our unqualified support and backing. From here on in you call your shots and we'll ride with you. Only—beat that deadline! Now I've had enough argument and I'm off for some supper.'

71

They filed out, Ames grinning, Leffingwell truculent, Henry Shard sour and tight-lipped. Bart Runnell was glowering. At last Luke and John Guthrie were alone.

Guthrie clasped both hands above his head and shook them in a gesture of victory. 'Luke,' he exulted, 'you're a genius! You called Shard's hand in just the right way and at the right time. He's such a damned stubborn old coot. I'll say the air is cleared!'

'On the contrary, John, there's still plenty of murk,' said Luke. 'And it's going to get thicker before it finally clears up. But that's neither here nor there. What we need now is action, for time is slipping away from us. I'm taking Joe Keller and his steel gang out to Corinth. I'm taking Dick Leslie along, too. You and Johnny Megarry stay at this end and build grade as fast as possible. We'll catch up with the steel later, if we all have to get out there and swing a spiking sledge, or grab a wrench and bolt up fish-plate. You might see Alec Craigie and have him ready to roll by daylight tomorrow. From here on in take nothing for granted from anybody. This outfit hasn't seen anything yet in the way of bombshells.'

Guthrie frowned, staring at him. 'You haven't told all you know, Luke.'

'And I won't until I'm a little more certain of things. But in the meantime, let's go! You see Joe Keller and Craigie and tell them what to line up. I'll see Johnny Megarry and Dick

Leslie.'

While eating his supper in Ma Megarry's kitchen, Luke gave Johnny Megarry the picture. Then, his pipe going, Luke headed for the Leslie cabin. At his knock, Dick Leslie opened the door and seized upon Luke excitedly. 'All kinds of rumors drifting around, Luke. Come in here and put me right about them. It's even in the air that we may have some steel coming up.'

'We have,' said Luke. 'And you're going out with me to help round it up.' Then Luke sketched briefly the story of the Corinth steel. While he spoke, Dale Leslie came in from another room of the cabin. Whooping boyishly, Dick caught his sister by the hands and spun her around.

'Hear that, Sis? Luke's rounded up some steel for us. We're going after it in the morning. I'll be needing some gear, of course. My sleeping bag is down at the construction office. I'm going after it. Be back in a jiffy, Luke.' And then, grabbing his hat and coat, Dick dashed out.

Left alone with the girl, Luke smiled gravely. 'Fine lad, that brother of yours, Miss Leslie. I like his enthusiasm.'

The girl's nod was almost curt. 'I hope it doesn't lead him into worshipping false gods.'

Luke's smile faded. He said bluntly, 'Why do you dislike me so? If you're still offended because of the way I watched you that day in

73

the caboose, coming in from Garnet, I'll say again that I am sorry and that I meant no offense.'

She colored faintly. 'I wasn't aware that I was interested one way or the other, Mr. Fenimore.'

If this wasn't a slap in the face it was very close to it. Luke's face hardened. 'Which just goes to show how appearances can deceive,' he said harshly. 'For behind your sheer loveliness there should be some gentleness.'

He saw the anger flare in her eyes and knew a wayward satisfaction over it. But before she could answer there was an abrupt, hard knock, then the door opened and Bart Runnell came in. His face was dark with seething emotion.

'So here you are, eh, Fenimore?' he exploded. 'Now you wouldn't be trying to build your little steel buccaneering scheme up into a triumph, would you?'

'Hardly,' rapped Luke curtly. 'But at least it means we get steel this trip instead of a shrug of the shoulder and a report of failure.'

The fury in Runnell's face deepened. 'Any time I have to turn damned thief to get steel, I don't want it.'

Lines of white bracketed Luke's lips. 'This is a good safe place to pull a crack like that Runnell. Try it again some time when we are not in a lady's house.'

Dale Leslie forestalled further retort by Runnell. 'What do you mean, Bart—about this steel question? Is there anything shady concerning it?'

Runnell barked a short laugh. 'Shady is putting it mildly, Dale. There is a narrow-gauge property out at Corinth on the main transcontinental line. Fenimore here has sold the idea to Ames and Leffingwell and Guthrie that we go out there and help ourselves. Take steel and rolling stock without so much as a by-your-leave from the owners—without even bothering to contact the owners, in fact. Henry Shard was the only one with decency enough to oppose such a highhanded business. Sure—just go and take it, along with a locomotive and a couple of flatcars. If that isn't thievery, I don't know what is!'

The girl looked at Luke. 'Well?'

'Runnell,' shrugged Luke, 'forgot to add that the property, to all visible intents and purposes, has long ago been abandoned. Also that we intend to pay for what we take once we locate the owners.'

'But you haven't contacted the owners—yet?'

'No, we haven't. We haven't had time to. But we must have steel to beat the subsidy deadline. We can't afford to stand on a lot of time-wasting ceremony. We've got to have that steel! And I'm quite sure that the owners, once we locate then, will be only too glad to get a little money out of something they have apparently long ago written off as a dead loss.'

'Never was a thief who couldn't find some excuse for his actions,' sneered Runnell.

Little knots of muscle stood out at the hard angles of Luke's jaw. But his voice went soft as silk. 'That's twice, Runnell. The third time you say it will be the payoff, regardless of whose house we are in or of who may be present. Watch yourself!'

Bart Runnell might have said it again, right then and there, had not Dick Leslie come hurrying back to the cabin, lugging a sleeping bag and other gear. His sister turned to him. 'You're not to go to Corinth, Dick. You stick to your own job—here. Let others go and take steel that doesn't belong to them.'

Dick stared at her, 'Sis! You're talking foolish. Of course I'm going to Corinth. Why shouldn't I?'

'Because Bart says we have no right to that steel. That to take it this way is stealing—no less.'

'Bosh!' exclaimed Dick heatedly. 'Bart's crazy! And if he'd show a little more enthusiasm—and results—getting things done, and less making excuses and criticizing others, I'd think more of him. Luke, I'll be ready to leave in the morning with you and Joe and the rest of the boys.'

'If you do it will be against my wishes,' said his sister.

'Dale's right, Dick,' put in Runnell. 'You don't want to have any part of this deal. It will only lead to trouble.'

Young Dick Leslie stood silent for a moment, his glance moving from his sister to Runnell. The line of his jaw turned taut. 'Sis, you're not thinking with your head, right now. Runnell, when and if I ever want your advice, or think that I need it, I'll ask for it. Until then, kindly keep out of anything that concerns Dale and me alone. Luke, I'll be with you in the morning.'

Luke smiled grimly. 'Good boy, Dick. Be seeing you.' He bowed slightly to the girl. 'Good night, Miss Leslie. Don't worry about your brother. I won't lead him astray.'

*   *   *

Joe Keller and his gang ripped up steel far faster than they had ever laid it down. The mechanics whom Warren Garland sent out to Corinth from the roundhouse at LeMoyne checked over the old Union Foundry engine and went to work. In a little less than a day they had it ready to go.

'To make her as she was once,' a grinning mechanic told Luke Fenimore, 'would take just about a complete rebuilding job, for which we've neither the equipment nor the parts. Yet she's ready to roll now, after a fashion. She'll squeak and she'll rattle and she'll do a heap of leaking at the seams. And she won't push a mountain down by a hell of a lot. Yet, such as she is, she ought to earn her keep. Good luck!'

Along the back trail of jobs Luke had worked at in his time had been a summer at the throttle of a switch engine in a freight yard. So the workings of the old Union Foundry job were not a complete mystery to him. With Dick Leslie firing, they made the old-timer go. With the two flats in front of them they pushed slowly out to the end of steel. There were places here and there where they had to stop and grub out sagebrush that had grown over the tracks. They filled washouts and bolstered up rotten ties. They held their collective breaths and waited for calamity to strike. They lurched and wobbled and clanked. They squeaked and rattled and squealed. But they got to the end of steel, where, as fast as it was ripped up, it was piled on the flats and hauled back to Corinth. Each trip progressively shortened the run.

When a full car of steel was piled at Corinth it was loaded onto a main-line flat and sent along to Garnet, there to be transferred to a Desert & Central narrow-gauge flat and hauled south to Cold Creek behind the Simcoe. They wasted not a minute of daylight, being on the job as soon as they could see in the morning, and staying with it as long as they could see at night. The cooks worked over open fires and the men ate and slept like siwashes in the old engine shed. They grew bearded and grimy and black, but they got out

78

that steel!

Rolling back to Corinth with still another load, Luke called across the cab above the wheezing labors of the old engine, 'One more full day and we'll have it all, Dick.'

Dick nodded and grinned. 'Don't know when I've had so much fun. This beats running levels and laying out grade stakes all hollow.'

They snorted out of the last fringe of sage and rolled to a stop at the main-line siding. Over by the sheds four saddled horses stood, shot-hipped and dozing. Now two strangers, who had been talking to the cooks, came sauntering over, eying Luke and Dick speculatively as they climbed down out of the cab.

'Howdy!' said the leader of the two strangers. 'Jing and me are deputies, working out of the sheriff's office at Viault. We're looking for a couple of gents, one named Fenimore, the other Leslie. Where'll we find 'em?'

'What do you want them for?' asked Luke guardedly.

'Well, there's a little matter of a court injunction to put a stop to this monkey business of snatching railroad steel. Then there are a couple of warrants for arrest.'

'Arrest for what?'

'What do you think? For stealing railroad equipment, of course. Now you two wouldn't happen to be Fenimore and Leslie, would

79

you?'

'There's no sense to one of those warrants,' Luke rapped. 'The one for Dick Leslie. He's just working for me.'

The deputy grinned thinly. 'You're Fenimore, I take it?'

'That's right.'

'And I'm Leslie,' put in Dick firmly. 'If you can arrest Luke, you can arrest me. I'm in this all the way, for better or worse.'

'Looks like it's for worse, partner,' the deputy drawled. 'All right, Jing—slap the cuffs on them!'

CHAPTER FOUR

THE BIGGER JOB

Jing, the second deputy, silent up until now, spat a stream of tobacco juice, pulled a set of handcuffs from his pocket and stepped up to Dick Leslie. 'Put out your mitts,' he said curtly.

'Sure,' said Dick, shoving out both hands.

Jing reached for one of Dick's wrists and the next deft second Dick had exploded into flashing movement. There was a blur of action, a shift of bodies and the next moment Jing was completely turned over in the air, to land with a crash on the broad of his shoulders, all the wind and wits knocked completely out of him.

Pike, the other deputy, blurted a curse and followed with a hand sweeping toward the shoulder-holstered gun he carried. He had the gun half drawn when Luke rolled his right shoulder behind a punch that found Pike's jaw with a hefty spat. Pike's legs went rubbery and he collapsed. As he fell, Luke grabbed the gun from his fingers.

Dick, who had followed Jing to the ground, now stood up, leaving Jing helpless in the grip of his own handcuffs. He located a pair of the same steel bonds in Pike's pocket and clamped them on their owner's wrists. Then he straightened up, looked at Luke and grinned cheerfully.

'More fun! But now we'll get the rest of that steel out.'

Luke said slowly, 'Boy—you surprise me. Just what the devil did you do to friend Jing, yonder? One second he was up, the next he was down—hard. But I didn't see you hit him.'

'Just a little old wristlock,' said Dick. 'In college I was rated a pretty fair middleweight wrestler.'

'Your sister,' said Luke gravely, 'will hate me forever. I promised her I wouldn't get you into trouble.'

Dick shrugged, 'Sis has a few old-fashioned ideas she's going to have to get rid of,' he declared. 'One of them is that her brother is a softy who has to be protected from the rough old world. Another thing she must come to understand is that I am not going to back out of the picture just because the going gets tough We've got a railroad to build, a deadline to beat and a quarter-million dollar subsidy to win. If we have to tangle with a few phony injunctions and arrest warrants to get the job done, then that's the way it will have to be, I guess.'

'Then you think these two lovely birds are phonies?'

'Who knows? We'll find out later, after we have the steel out and the equipment on its way.'

Luke dropped a hand on Dick's shoulder, gripped it tight. 'You'll do to cross the tracks with, any old time. You know, Dick, I half suspected something like this might turn up. Which is the reason I brought you out here in the first place. So you could take over the job and carry it along, in case they lugged me off to a lockup. But it would seem now that somebody else was foxy and saw through my little scheme. So they aimed to put you right alongside of me behind those bars.'

By this time the two deputies had regained their wits and breath. They struggled to their feet and Pike snarled, 'You two smart jingoes will wish you'd never been born, pulling a deal like this. Resisting the law ain't something that folks get away with easy in these parts. When the judge gets through with you, you won't stack up as bein' half as smart as you think.'

'We'll worry about that when the time comes,' drawled Luke. 'Right now we're too busy to bother. You two are going to be our guests for a couple of days while we finish a job we got to do. We're not trying to beat the arrests. We're just postponing them for a little while. When our job is done, we'll trot right along with you two to Viault. In the meantime, all you got to do is lay around and take life easy. The cooks will look after you.'

The two cooks, or more rightly, the cook and his helper, had viewed the happenings with considerable amazement and alarm, but when Luke explained matters to them, they grinned and nodded. 'Leave 'em here, boss,' said the cook. 'We'll keep an eye on them for you. Just can't have anybody stop us from getting out our steel.'

'Your steel!' blurted Pike. 'Why, you damned thieves—'

The cook brandished a frying pan. 'You,' he growled, 'shut up! Any more of your lip and I pat you in the face with this pan—and hard!'

Pike and Jing subsided, surly and glowering.

When Luke and Dick got back to where Joe Keller and the gang were working, Luke told Joe what had happened. 'Pass the word on to the boys, Joe. We've got to get the job done before they come out to see what's happened to their deputies.'

The word went out and the tempo of the job picked up. Through the crew of a westbound

83

main-line local freight that stopped to hook on a flat of steel, Luke sent a brief message to Warren Garland at LeMoyne and around midmorning of the following day, an engine, some flats and a wrecking crane came rolling up the main line and pulled in on the Corinth siding. Warren Garland climbed down out of the engine cab and sauntered over to where Luke and Dick had just pulled in with their two little flats piled high with the precious narrow-gauge steel.

Warren Garland grinned at Luke. 'Got yourselves into a peck of trouble, eh? Well, I wouldn't worry too much. While the lawyers argue your crowd can be laying steel, which is all that counts, now. Chances are you won't have to spend too much time behind bars.' He looked the old Union Foundry engine over. 'Durned little teakettle runs doesn't it?'

'Sure thing,' chuckled Luke. 'She's a honey. Want to try her?'

Warren Garland took the throttle for the next short run. He was like a little boy out of school. He grinned and chuckled and his eyes shone. Once he jerked his head back toward Corinth and shouted above the complaining labors of the old engine, 'Back there on the main line some of the proudest trains in America are rolling over some of the finest roadbed. But I'd rather be right here hogging this old wreck along than at the throttle of one of those prize Moguls. Hell! This brings back a man's youth.'

The job closed out fast. By four o'clock that afternoon all the steel was up and loaded, even the old siding. A few yards of track were slapped down, just enough to roll the little old engine and the two flats within reach of the wrecking crane. That powerful gear, used to tugging and lifting at big, main-liner stuff, made short work of swinging the Union Foundry engine and the two little flats up onto a couple of the big, main-line flats, where their wheels were blocked and lashed down.

Luke drew a deep breath. 'That's that! Take 'em away. Joe Keller, it's in your hands now. We'll be seeing you again shortly, I hope. Right now Dick Leslie and I've got to keep a date with a judge over in Viault.'

'So have I,' drawled Warren Garland. 'There are a few things that I grow more and more curious about. Now don't try and argue, Luke. Didn't I tell you I was having fun? I'll be seeing you in Viault.'

Luke and Dick went over to the two deputies, who had watched the final closing out of the Corinth steel job with sulky eyes. Also, the presence of Warren Garland, whose identity they seemed well aware of, filled them with a certain dubious uncertainty. Luke unlocked the cuffs from the wrists of Pike and Jing and threw the offending manacles out into the sage, with the key following.

'All right,' he said. 'We'll go along with you

now. But we're not wearing cuffs. No hard feelings, you understand, gents. It's all been just the workings of necessity.'

The disgruntled Pike mumbled, 'You can tell all that to the judge. He may change your minds on certain things.'

Luke shrugged. 'That may be, but at least we got the steel. Let's go!'

Up on the two spare horses the deputies had brought along, Luke and Dick rode east with their captors, paralleling the main-line right of way. At dark they cut northeast and some two hours later rode into the town of Viault. With obvious relish the deputies led them into a dingy little sheriff's office where a dumpy man with fat jowls lolled at ease behind a small desk.

'Here they are, Bid,' said Pike. 'And along with the original charges we got plenty of others. Resisting an officer and—'

Sheriff Bid Harpe waved a stubby arm and grunted. 'Save your breath. They're already out on bail. Judge Whorly and that big boss from the railroad, Garland, just left here about half an hour ago. You two'—and he looked at Luke and Dick Leslie—'are to go up to the hotel. You'll find Garland waiting there for you.'

Warren Garland was sitting in the lobby of the ramshackle little hotel and he grinned at Luke and Dick as they entered. 'Well, how do you two terrible criminals feel now, as wards of

86

the law, so to speak?'

'All right and plenty thankful to you,' answered Luke. 'I don't know how we'll ever be able to thank you—'

'Save it,' broke in Warren Garland, eyes twinkling. 'I imagine your first concern is food. And if you two want to take out time to eat, you'll have to spend the night in this joint. But if you're willing to go hungry for a while we can just about make it back to Cherry Meadows in time to grab a westbound midnight freight. Which will it be?'

'I'd rather eat breakfast in Garnet,' said Luke.

Dick Leslie nodded. 'Same here.'

'Then we go,' said Garland.

Warren Garland had a buckboard and team that he had driven into Viault from Cherry Meadows. The team had plenty of go to it and the buckboard whisked swiftly along the narrow road through the sage. They beat the midnight freight into Cherry Meadows by a full five minutes and when they climbed into the caboose of the freight, Luke said, 'I hope the Desert & Central someday is able to vote a dividend in your name, Mr. Garland.'

Warren Garland smiled. 'Railroads—big and little—interest me. So do the men who build them—and the men who try and keep them from being built. Luke, don't you take a thing for granted from here on in. You got more to whip than just time and distance.

There are angles cropping up in this deal that intrigue me no end. Something is rotten in the sagebrush, and I'm beginning to smell it. For instance, suppose I was to tell you that the man who signed the injunction and arrest complaints against you and Leslie was the same man who brought up that Grasshopper steel.'

'Fargo?' breathed Luke.

'Fargo!'

'Now that you say it, it doesn't surprise me at all,' said Luke. 'Quite the busy little bee, isn't he? But you wouldn't tell me, though, that he's owned the Corinth steel all this time. And he would have to, to sign that injunction and swear out the arrest warrants.'

'He owns just five shares of stock,' said Garland. 'Seems that the old White Queen Mine, to which the Corinth steel was to reach, was a stock-company holding. It happened that Judge Whorly, an old friend of mine, could recall some of the history of the mine. Somehow and somewhere this fellow Fargo got hold of enough shares to put that injunction across. For that matter, one share would have been enough.'

'I'm wondering,' mused Luke, 'if Desert & Central could have luck enough to pick up a few of those old shares—enough to quash that injunction, which would more or less automatically put Dick Leslie and me in the clear again? It might be a good idea to try, or there could still be trouble thrown our way at a later and even more critical time.'

Warren Garland nodded. 'My own thought. So, first thing tomorrow morning I'm going to get in touch with our legal staff at Reno and have all the records of the White Queen Mine run down. If possible, I'll have them locate some of the other stockholders, in which case it should not be too difficult to get hold of enough stock to quash the injunction. No doubt the stock is dirt-cheap, and whoever holds any of it will probably be only too glad to realize even a dime on a dollar out of it when up to now it has plainly been virtually worthless. I'll let you people know all about it just as soon as I can run the information down. In the meantime you and Leslie are out on bail and you can get ahead with the job of beating that deadline and winning the subsidy. We'll see about the rest in our own good time.'

*   *   *

With Luke Fenimore at the throttle and Dick Leslie firing, the Union Foundry engine hauled the last two flats of Corinth steel from Garnet to Cold Creek. The old engine was hard put to it to get over Rockaway Pass, but Luke knew her peculiarities now, and he nursed her over. And when he came rolling down into Cold Creek the old girl squealed her whistle triumph under a banner of trailing steam.

John Guthrie, among others, was there to meet them. He looked ten years younger. He patted the scabbed and scarred giltwork on the cab of the old engine. 'It might be junk to some, but it is pure gold to us!" he exclaimed. 'Luke, this is wonderful!'

'It took a little longer than I figured, John,' said Luke soberly. 'We've had our troubles and they'd have been really bad ones if it hadn't been for Warren Garland. There is one white man! Now we've got a lot of time to make up.'

Guthrie laughed, 'Did you think we'd be sleeping at this end? Say, you don't know Johnny Megarry—or Johnny Guthrie, either. We're six miles out from where you saw us last, with Corinth steel laid on every foot of it. Johnny Megarry and his gang have been tremendous—doing double duty. Half a day they would build grade. The other half they laid steel. Now, with Joe Keller and his gang back with us, we'll really cover ground. Still more good news. Frank Ames sends word that he and Curt Leffingwell have got action at the mills. New steel will begin arriving within another week. Which means that it will hit here just about the time we'll be needing it. This Corinth steel has bridged the gap, Luke. And when we whip that deadline, it will be Corinth steel that really did the job.'

Luke, looking around for Dick Leslie, saw Dick talking to his sister, Dale. The girl's head was high and her face pale, except for a spot of crimson on either cheek, while her eyes were bright with anger. Obviously she was lathering Dick about something and Dick was making rather heavy going of it as he tried to explain. Abruptly the girl swung her head and looked at Luke, then came swiftly over to him.

'So!' she lashed, her voice low and tense. 'You wouldn't lead Dick astray, wouldn't you! You wouldn't get him into trouble. Oh, no— not a bit of it! But it seems he was arrested, along with you, like any other common thief. Now he tells me he is out on bail—on bail! There is no telling where—or what this may lead to. It might even mean the—the penitentiary for Dick! And you gave me your word!' She broke off, blinking rapidly, her eyes brimming and her lips taut and stiff. 'Bart— Bart was right. But just because you have the instincts of a thief, you needn't have led Dick into the same dirty category.'

'Wait a minute, Miss Leslie!' Luke's voice was curt, flat, a little weary. 'I'm sorry about Dick. But they haven't a thing against the boy, any more than they have against Joe Keller or any of the men who worked at tearing up the steel. And Dick is under no more threat of going to prison than you are. The whole fuss is more one of technicalities than anything else. And I say to you, instead of rawhiding Dick, you should be proud of him. For I am. That boy is all wool and a yard wide. So don't go

91

throwing that word "thief" around too much. For someday you may be sorry. Call me what you want, but don't include Dick in it. He deserves better than that from you. Now, if you'll excuse me—'

He turned and walked away, his shoulders very straight. He stopped in at the general store and bought a complete new outfit of clothes, for those that he had were in tatters. That Corinth steel job had been hard on clothes as well as on men. At Ma Megarry's boardinghouse he had a shave, a hot bath, then donned his new outfit.

A slow, deep anger was burning in Luke, some of it at Dale Leslie. He'd had about all that thief talk he could stand, even from her. It would, he thought, be damned dangerous for anyone to use the word against him again.

He couldn't understand that girl. There was so much about her that was deep and fine and intelligent, so much that had got hold of him and drew him and made her the symbol of all that was best in life to him. Now, bitterly, he tried to tell himself that it didn't really matter what she thought of him and that he didn't really care a damn.

The next moment, staring at the wall, he muttered softly, 'That won't do, Fenimore. Never before in your life have you tried to kid yourself, so why start now? You know that it does matter what she thinks of you. It matters just about more than anything ever mattered before in your life. And you care—plenty! And she's got no more use for you than she has for anyone else with the instincts of a thief. That hurt, Fenimore. I hope you never bump into anything that hurts you more.'

He went back down to the tracks and found, to his surprise, Dick Leslie waiting there, busy with an oilcan around the old Union Foundry engine. Dick's face was grim, sterner than Luke had ever seen it. 'I figured you'd want to get out to the end of steel to see how things were going,' said Dick. 'Shall we roll?'

So they did roll, snaking along the two flats of steel. They found the Simcoe out there, pushing up several carloads of ties. Alec Craigie and Casey O'Keefe got down, came back and walked up and down beside the Union Foundry job, looking it over.

'And what would you call it, Alec?' grinned Casey. 'Is it an engine or an animated teakettle?'

'I'm wondering,' twinkled Craigie. 'I see a wheel or two on it. But then even a pushcart's got wheels.'

'Don't you two hooligans go throwing bricks at old Betsy Ann,' said Luke. 'She's creaky in the joints and has a fine case of asthma. But once she was a grand lady and she sure shapes up as a lifesaver for us. You better get used to her, Casey. For from now on you'll be hogging her. You're no longer firing. You've got a throttle of your own to handle.'

93

'Ha!' snorted Alec Craigie. 'Ha! Now won't they make a great pair. This old bucket of rust and the great O'Keefe himself!'

Casey bristled. 'Go easy on your blackguardin', ye Scotch scut. Now that I take a second look at her, she's got the lines of a thoroughbred. I'm thinkin' that with O'Keefe to coddle her and give her a bit of Christian care, she'll have you and the Simcoe humping plenty to keep out of her way. Now you'll be giving me a hand at polishing up her brasswork and greasing some of the misery out of her joints or it'll be the worse for you, my fine and scornful friend.'

Leaving Alec and Casey to argue and blackguard each other while checking over the old engine with expert hand and eye, Luke and Dick footed it out to where Johnny Megarry and his gang were building grade in a clatter of industry. Johnny looked a bit leaned about the mouth and jaw, but his good-natured grin broke as Luke and Dick came up to him.

'You big slab-sided mick,' growled Luke. 'What have you been trying to do, work yourself and your crew to death?'

Johnny's honest eyes gleamed. 'Didn't I tell you once, Luke, that there was nothing wrong with the boys? Now didn't I? Well, they're not terriers any more. They're wolves for work and they keep me jumpin' to stay out in front of them. The boys, they figured that if the rest of you could go get steel, then they could lay it as well as build the grade.'

'Had you been just half this far along, I'd have said "well done," Johnny,' Luke said simply.

Johnny arched his big chest. 'When you got the men, the tools, the steel, and as sweet a job of surveying as Dick here has turned out, why then the road fair builds itself.'

Luke and Dick spent the balance of the day out at end of construction. About an hour before quitting time a two-seater buckboard came rolling along the freight road, to pull off and stop beside the job. Curt Leffingwell was driving and with him were Frank Ames and Henry Shard. The three of them got out and came over.

'This,' said Frank Ames heartily, 'amazes me, Fenimore. You're miles out from Cold Creek, already.'

Luke said, 'The boys have been putting out, Mr. Ames.'

'And this is Corinth steel?' asked Curt Leffingwell.

Luke nodded. 'All of it. Six miles of it already laid and we've enough for another six. By that time, so John Guthrie tells me, we can expect our new steel to begin arriving.'

'That's right. We finally got things moving at the mills. How did that old locomotive work out?'

'Fine. It's back yonder. Casey O'Keefe will be hogging it. He and Craigie can both break in new men for firing. And I suggest we keep the old Union Foundry rig on this side of Rockaway Pass, just to handle things for the construction gangs, bringing up steel and ties, taking the men back and forth and such necessary chores. Which will leave the Simcoe free to handle everything between Cold Creek and Garnet.'

'That makes sense,' nodded Leffingwell. 'Run things to suit yourself Luke. You're getting action, which is what we want. Runnell around?'

'Haven't seen him. Megarry would know. Hi, Johnny—is Bart Runnell around?'

Johnny shook his head. 'He hasn't been around today. Nor yesterday, either.'

Henry Shard spoke, his voice harsh and thinly twanging. 'Bart has plenty of other things on his mind than just watching a bunch of railroad jerries swing a pick and shovel or push on the handle of a Fresno scraper.'

'Apparently,' said Leffingwell dryly.

The three mineowners hung around for a little while, watching the work. Frank Ames and Curt Leffingwell were plainly highly pleased with the progress being made. Even Henry Shard, stubborn and cantankerous and at no pains to mask his dislike of Luke, gave grudging approval. 'This is a good showing,' he conceded. 'But maybe we won't be so proud of it if, later on, we find ourselves facing a ruinous lawsuit over this Corinth steel.'

'Henry,' jibed Frank Ames, 'you'd kick if your shirt-tail was on fire.'

Frank Ames and Henry Shard went over to the buckboard, but Curt Leffingwell lingered a moment. 'We'll be having another meeting in Guthrie's room this evening, Luke,' he said. 'Better drop around. We may have something rather interesting to tell you.'

Luke nodded. 'I'll be there. For I've something interesting to relate, myself.'

Leffingwell looked at him narrowly. 'Not playing with the idea again of quitting us, I hope?'

Luke smiled slightly, shaking his head. 'Nothing like that. But it won't leave you sleeping any better of nights.'

Leffingwell waved a hand. 'Just so you're not going to quit. Be seeing you, then.'

He went over, got into the buckboard and drove on toward Cold Creek.

A little later, when he and Dick Leslie were alone, Luke brought up again the thing that was hammering at the back of his mind. 'I wish now that I hadn't taken you out to Corinth with me, Dick. Your sister is pretty badly upset over our trouble with those deputies from Viault.'

Dick was grimly silent for a moment. Then he said, 'Dale is a grand sister. But in some ways she's been spoiled. Being older than I am, she naturally figures she's got to look out for me. I've humored her a great deal that way in the past. But it's high time that she realize I'm not a baby any longer. The main trouble, I think, is that she's let Bart Runnell and his talk scare her half to death. I'm sure going to tell Runnell a thing or two the next time I see him.'

'I don't want to be the cause of any family trouble for you Dick,' said Luke. 'But it seems I have been.'

'No!' declared Dick, 'you haven't. What if I did get arrested? What if I am out on bail? The cause was legitimate and I can't think of a better one. My job isn't just running surveys and setting up grade stakes, nor is it just drawing up plans for the four bridges to cross Castle River and any other odds and ends of engineering the job calls for. None of that will amount to a thing unless the job as a whole is put across and put across right—the deadline beat and the subsidy won. Which is exactly what I told Dale. And if I have to get arrested again to help whip the main, all-over job, why then I'll get arrested.'

'That's the proper spirit, of course,' Luke said quietly. 'But just the same, don't you go quarreling with your sister. I'd never forgive myself if I was the cause of any real trouble between you two.'

Dick laughed, slapping Luke on the shoulder. 'Don't worry about that. There'll never be any real trouble between Dale and me. We're much too fond of each other for that. But a little lesson won't do Sis a bit of harm. I wish though—' Dick paused, frowned, then shrugged. 'Oh, well—everything will be all right.'

CHAPTER FIVE

HATRED'S EDGE

When Luke Fenimore arrived at John Guthrie's hotel room that evening it was evident that the meeting had already been in heated session for some time. Henry Shard was glowering and sour, Curt Leffingwell looked hard-boiled, while Frank Ames was merely imperturbable. John Guthrie had a gleam of quiet satisfaction in his eyes.

Curt Leffingwell wasted little time in setting off a bombshell. 'We're making a change, Fenimore,' he said. 'You're the new Construction Superintendent, if you'll take the job. I hope you will.'

Luke stood still, looking around. 'Well, gentlemen—this is a real surprise. Sort of takes me off my feet, so to speak. I hardly expected anything like this.'

Leffingwell shrugged. 'No sense in beating around the bush. There has been far too much dilly-dallying on important issues already. How about it? Do you want the job?'

'Being human, of course I do. But what about Runnell?'

'Devil take Bart Runnell!' exploded the forthright Curt Leffingwell. 'I'm thoroughly fed up with that fellow. He's let us down all along the line. He let the grade gang get out of hand, which completely tied up the work. We sent him after that Grasshopper steel and he fell down there, too. And from all I can learn, he didn't seem a bit put out over his failure. Next, while you were away at Corinth, working night and day to get us the steel we absolutely had to have, and with John Guthrie and Megarry and the grade gang doing double duty and a damn fine job of it too, where was Mr. Bartley Runnell? Was he on the job, doing his part? Hardly. He wasn't even interested enough to show up on construction. I don't know where he was or what he was doing. But I do know that he was doing nothing in our interest. So he is done—through! And the job he had is yours.'

'Has he been notified?' asked Luke.

'Not yet, but he soon will be. We've sent Joe Keller to round him up and bring him here.'

Luke looked around again. Henry Shard was staring at him with gimlet eyes. It was a queer look, but plainly one of open dislike. Which was a little hard to understand. As far as Luke knew, he had never done the man a wrong in his life. The only answer to arrive at was that Shard had it in for him because of their argument over the Corinth steel, an argument Luke had won. In any event, it was plain to see that the new job had come through the insistence of Curt Leffingwell and Frank Ames, with no doubt a boost from John Guthrie. Whatever his reasons, it was evident that Henry Shard did not approve.

Steps sounded in the hall outside and the door opened to let in Bart Runnell. It seemed that Runnell sensed what was in the air. Though he moved with his usual faint suggestion of a swagger, his glance darted about, questioning and uneasy. When he spoke it was with a forced heartiness.

'Gentlemen! You wanted to see me?'

'Yes,' Leffingwell told him bluntly. 'Yes, we do. A question or two, Runnell. Just what have you been busy at the past few days—so busy that you couldn't bother to get out on construction and see how things were going?'

Leffingwell's words were no more blunt and insistent than his boring glance, and under the impact of it Runnell flushed, and fumbled somewhat for words. 'Why—er—this and that. Several things I wanted to clean up.'

'This and that, eh?' said Leffingwell dryly. 'Apparently anything and everything except the railroad business for which you were originally hired. I don't believe the job is big enough or means enough to you any more—not enough for you to continue at it. So, effective immediately, we are letting you go.'

It was terse and blunt and direct, but that was Curt Leffingwell's way.

The flush in Runnell's face deepened until it was a blaze of anger, pulling his handsome features into something almost like a snarl. 'So-o!' he gritted. 'That's it, eh? Somebody seems to have been selling me down the river, cutting things from under me behind my back. Guthrie, maybe—or more likely, Mr. Luke Fenimore?'

Curt Leffingwell waved his arm in a short, scoffing gesture. 'Any selling down the river was done by yourself, Runnell. Don't try and pass the buck to someone else. You yourself are entirely responsible. This job calls for action, for the ability to get things done. And you didn't produce. So, we had to get someone who could.'

'And that person, no doubt,' sneered Runnell, 'is, of course, Luke Fenimore?'

'That's right—Luke Fenimore,' said Leffingwell shortly. 'Your check, Runnell, will be drawn up to the fifteenth of the month which is more than fair and better than you deserve. That's all.'

'No! It's not all. It's not even a small part of it, as you'll damn well find out before you get through—before your damned dinky railroad gets—' Runnell broke off, choking back his fury by distinct effort. He swung around to face Luke, his head thrust forward, his features working. 'There'll be a reckoning between you

102

and me, Fenimore—a big reckoning. Through, am I? We'll see!'

He whirled then and went out, closing the door behind him with a slam which must have loosened the hinges. Curt Leffingwell reached in his pocket for a cheroot, bit the end off it, lighted it and said calmly, 'So much for that. I never did like to fire a man, unless I considered the move absolutely necessary. In this case it was. Now then, Luke, you said something this afternoon about having something of a bombshell of your own to set off. Let's have it.'

Luke nodded. 'Very well. The picture I got of this job before I became a part of it was something like this. From Garnet to Cold Creek the job went along in fine style, even to the part over Rockaway Pass which stacks up definitely as the toughest stretch of all. But, after getting as far as Cold Creek, things began to happen. Everything seemed to go wrong at once. Did the thought ever strike you, gentlemen, that there might have been more to all those sudden difficulties than just pure coincidence?'

Curt Leffingwell's cheroot tilted upward at the corner of his mouth and through the smoke of it he flashed Luke a hard, unreadable glance. 'Go on,' he growled.

'Well,' said Luke, 'the first day I came in to Cold Creek, the Simcoe was pulling a pretty heavy load from Garnet. When we topped out over Rockaway we stopped for water at the tower at Kicking Horse. Three tough ones, with "mule skinner" written all over them, came into the caboose. They were looking for me, they said. Their declared intention was to hustle me off the train and send me packing, clear out of this part of the country. As it happened, they were a little short on the necessary authority to put over what they intended. Later, after we went on, the brakeman told me that these same three had been hanging around Kicking Horse for several days and made a habit, every time the train stopped for water, of coming into the caboose and looking things over, quite evidently waiting and watching for me to show up. The brakeman also identified one of the three as a skinner he'd seen handling one of Jack Fargo's freight outfits.'

'In other words,' remarked Frank Ames, 'you are suggesting, Luke, that those three mule skinners had been stationed under orders from someone, to see that you never reached Cold Creek?'

'I can't see any other explanation,' shrugged Luke.

'Egotistical nonsense!' snorted Henry Shard thinly. 'You are trying to tell us that you consider yourself of such importance that you believe someone went to all that trouble to keep you out of Cold Creek?' His words dripped with sarcasm. 'I'd say you overrated yourself and your importance by a big margin, Fenimore.'

'Perhaps,' said Luke steadily. 'I've told you what happened. If you have a better explanation, I'd be interested in hearing it.'

'Shut up, Henry!' growled Curt Leffingwell bluntly. 'Keep your damned sarcasm to yourself. Go on, Luke.'

'Well, that's only part of it,' Luke said. 'Here is some more. The outfit that beat us to the Grasshopper steel calls itself the Western Mining Syndicate. And the man who acted in their behalf and tied up the steel so we couldn't get it, is named—Fargo!'

Here was the bombshell Luke had promised. Curt Leffingwell, Frank Ames and John Guthrie jumped as though a gun had gone off in the room. 'Fargo!' rapped Leffingwell. 'Could that be Jack Fargo?'

Luke, smiling thinly, shrugged. 'You guess. Now, something else. While we were getting out that Corinth steel, a pair of deputies showed up, armed with an injunction and a couple of arrest warrants, issued through a judge in Viault. The warrants were drawn against Dick Leslie and me. When the deputies went to arrest Dick and me, we sort of persuaded them to sit in a corner and be good dogs. Which they did until the job was finished and the steel and equipment were rolling this way. Then we went along with them to Viault.'

Frank Ames began to sputter. 'How—how the devil did you and Leslie get out of that jackpot? Curt and I didn't know anything about this. Why didn't you get word to us?'

'Didn't have to,' smiled Luke. 'Warren Garland sat into the picture and put up bail for Dick and me. He also found out who the man was who pushed the injunction and swore out those warrants. I'll give you one guess who it was.'

'Fargo!' exploded Leffingwell.

'No other. Jack Fargo.' Then Luke went on to tell them how Warren Garland had found out that Jack Fargo owned five shares in the old White Queen Mine and how Garland was having the legal staff of his railroad locate the other White Queen stockholders.

'You gentlemen will probably be served with a bill for the price of the stock Mr. Garland rounds up,' Luke ended. 'At the most it shouldn't amount to much in the way of money. And it will be enough stock to quash that injunction and put a halter on Fargo's maneuverings as a minority stockholder. In the meantime. Dick Leslie and I are free to keep the job rolling. I might add, gentlemen, that they don't come any finer than Warren Garland.'

'You're more than right, there,' said Curt Leffingwell. 'Now all this definitely adds up to just one answer. For some reason, Jack Fargo doesn't want us to beat that deadline. But why? His business is dependent upon our business.'

'Up to a point,' suggested Luke. 'Only up to a point. Look at it this way. Right now Jack Fargo holds about as fat a freighting contract as any man ever had. Which is, of course, doing all of the hauling between Cold Creek and Castle Mountain. He has that beautiful setup in which his wagons are loaded both going and coming. Food and supplies for the mines going in, a load of lead coming out. I don't know what his monthly bill to you people amounts to, but it must be plenty.'

'I'll say it's plenty!' growled Leffingwell. 'It's so much it constitutes the main reason why we're building this railroad. Not that he is overcharging us as freighting costs go in this country. He isn't. Frank and Henry and I checked on that pretty carefully some time ago. It's simply that our freight costs by mule team and wagon are so high, that it makes it worth our while, in the long-term view, to build a railroad. Your point, Luke, is, of course, that the day steel rails reach Castle Mountain, Fargo is out one mighty rich hunk of business.'

'That's right,' nodded Luke. 'I might add that the other evening I happened to look into the Big Sage saloon as I passed by, and there was Fargo having a very serious talk with those two old friends of ours, Bole Ives and Cob Ogard.'

107

Frank Ames, his head cocked on one side like an alert bird, murmured, 'A little angle which, if followed through, could lead to all sorts of conclusions. It could lead to none other than Mr. Bartley Runnell, who has but lately left our employ. When we add up Runnell's record for not getting things done, plus the fact that he made no effort to clean up the grade gang, where Ives and Ogard held forth, we come to—'

'That'll be enough of such talk, Ames,' cut in Henry Shard waspishly, 'Bart's been fired, and I'm not saying he didn't deserve it. But I want no surmising or hinting of dirty work on his part, when there isn't a single iota of proof of such. Let's put it down that Bart's been a little spoiled and that he took advantage of my good nature. For your information, Bart Runnell is my nephew, and as such I'll not have him blackguarded by anyone.'

Frank Ames' chin dropped. 'Your nephew? Why didn't you say so before?'

Henry Shard shrugged. 'I didn't want him shown any favors. I wanted him to stand on his own two feet. It was the agreement he and I had when he hit me up for the job—that our relationship was not to be disclosed to anyone.'

'I recall now that it was you who recommended him to Frank and me, Henry,' said Curt Leffingwell.

'Yes, I did,' admitted Shard. 'I was willing to

108

go that far for him, but I insisted that our relationship be kept secret, as I wanted no talk of favoritism to get around. Call it all a mistake and close the book. But no more name calling. We have far more serious disclosures to think about.'

'I'll say we have!' exploded Curt Leffingwell, pacing up and down the room, his eyes ashine with anger. 'It's high time we began putting this and that together. Fargo! Why, damn his conniving soul! We ought to cut him and his freighting contract right off at the pockets. Only—we can't.'

'No, we can't,' said John Guthrie, a silent and intent listener up to now. 'Fargo's running about fifty wagons. It takes about six hundred mules to keep those wagons rolling. Where could we locate someone else with the necessary equipment to take over at short notice in case we broke with Fargo? We couldn't, not in any reasonable space of time. Our only answer is to keep rooting and keep on laying steel. We'll meet and copper Fargo's tricks as we go along.'

'That's the only answer, John,' agreed Leffingwell. 'You and Luke play your own cards your own way and know that we'll back you through hell and high water. If anybody starts to play too rough, give it back to them with interest. From here on in anyone who deliberately gets in our way will wish that they'd never heard of us.'

*   *   *

Luke Fenimore would have been less than human if he hadn't known exultation over his promotion. He had been in construction long enough to know that the size of a man's position on a new job was almost always in direct relation to the importance of his last one. Reputation counted, and carried far. He had, he mused, come a long way since the day when, as a stripling kid, he had started as a roustabout and general Handy Andy with a survey gang.

He knew full well that he was being handed a tough assignment. He knew also that it wouldn't be enough just to come close. He had to beat that deadline. If he failed, it would hold him back. For in construction you don't come close. Either you did the job, or you didn't.

Thinking back over the explosive conference he had just left, Luke felt at last that he understood the source of Henry Shard's antagonism. Shard resented the way he had shown up Bart Runnell. The disclosure of this relationship between Shard and Runnell had been as big a surprise to Luke as it had to any of the others, but it definitely furnished the answer to one angle that Luke had wondered about. Whether Shard's attitude would be different in the future was

110

problematical.

Walking back through the night toward Ma Megarry's, Luke's mind ran ahead over the job. The grade gang was rolling now, and the steel was there to go down behind them. But there were other angles, such as four bridges to be built and ready when the steel came to them. Dick Leslie was handling the bridge job and Luke knew he had to have a clear picture in his mind how far bridge construction was along. In a sudden decision he turned toward the Leslie cabin.

This meant that in all probability he would meet Dale Leslie; and, in view of the way she obviously felt about him, such a meeting would be anything but pleasant. Yet, as the job progressed, it was inevitable that he should work more closely with Dick Leslie. So he couldn't let the attitude of the young construction engineer's sister stand in his way.

Lights were aglow in the cabin and when Luke knocked it was Dick who opened the door. Dick's jaw was set and the sparkle of anger was in his eyes. Intuition touched Luke and he said quickly, 'If I'm butting into something I shouldn't, Dick—just say so. I can see you tomorrow.'

'No! I'm glad you're here. Come on in!'

Luke stepped through the door and saw, across the table from him, Dale Leslie and Bart Runnell. There was anger and strain all through the room. Dick closed the door emphatically and said curtly, 'All right, Runnell! Here's Luke now. Let's hear you say it to his face.'

Runnell, seeming to be somewhat taken back, was silent for a moment. Not so the girl. She blazed at her brother. 'Dick! What in the world has come over you? Is this sort of thing necessary?'

'I think so,' was Dick's blunt answer. 'Frankly, I'm fed up with having a friend of mine constantly accused and maligned in my own home by Bart Runnell. And just as frankly, Sis, I'm not proud of you in being ready to accept Runnell's word so completely in all these things. Luke, you're being accused by Runnell of having undermined him— framed him were the exact words he used—so you could get his job. I don't believe it!'

'Thanks Dick,' said Luke quietly. 'No, I didn't frame him, or undermine him, either. He did that himself. After all, we have a railroad to build, a deadline to beat and a subsidy to win. The powers that be simply came to feel that Runnell failed to understand how serious and vital things have become. So, they let him out.'

'And gave you the job!' flared Dale Leslie.

Luke looked at her gravely, levelly. 'Yes. They gave me the job.'

'It was all cut and dried when I stepped into Guthrie's room,' charged Runnell, his eyes sultry. 'Don't tell me you hadn't been—'

'I am telling you,' Luke cut in. 'When they called me in and told me I was the new Construction Super I was completely surprised. They told me that before I had a chance to say a word.'

'And you accepted?'

'Naturally. Why shouldn't I? I owe you nothing, Runnell. In this construction game a man stands on his own two feet. He either makes good or he doesn't. I'm not working for my health. I'm working to get ahead the same as any other sane person. The fact that I've been given your job is your fault, not mine. You had your chance to make good.'

Anger distorted Bart Runnell's face. 'You got my job by being a damned thief. By stealing that Corinth—'

'That's plenty, Runnell. Twice before you called me a thief. I warned you then that the third time would be the payoff. Now you'll step outside and back up your words, or you'll take them back and apologize. Dick, I'm sorry. The last thing in the world I ever wanted to do was start an argument in your home, or in front of your sister. But there is a limit and I'm way past mine. Runnell steps outside with me, or I drag him out!'

Luke's face was white and cold, his voice shaky with feeling. Little knots of muscle were crawling and quivering along his bleak jaw.

'That's quite all right, Luke,' said Dick Leslie simply. 'Go the limit. In your place I'd do the same. All right, Runnell—you've been invited to step outside. Now we'll see whether you're just all lip and nothing else.'

Dale Leslie's face had gone very pale. She darted around and faced Luke. 'No!' she cried. 'No! I won't have it! This isn't necessary—this sort of thing. It isn't worthy!'

Her words choked off before the chill in Luke's eyes. It was as though he was looking at her from a tremendous distance. 'I'm sorry,' he said bleakly, 'but this is the way it must be. All right, Runnell—do you walk out or do I drag you out?'

Bart Runnell ejaculated a mumbled curse, plunged out of the house and Luke prowled after him. And Runnell, from the dark, getting Luke against the light, smashed a sudden and savage blow, full into Luke's face.

Runnell was a big man. He had square, heavy shoulders and he knew how to hit. The punch knocked Luke flat on his back, half in, half out of the door of the Leslie cabin. The blow dazed Luke, brought a smear of crimson from his lips. A lesser man might have stayed down and the fight been over with that single blow.

But back along the rough, tough trail of life, Luke Fenimore had learned many lessons. One was that a single knockdown did not win or lose a fight. A lot of things in life were like that. You had to get up off the floor again and again and keep on getting up, or you were washed out, quick! Washed out and left beside the trail while better men passed you by. So Luke got up, tasting his own blood, shaking his head to clear the numbing daze from it.

Instinct was at work there and it was instinct that made him weave and duck and cover up. And so it was that he avoided the savage flurry of blows which Bart Runnell, in a surge of defiant exultant fury, rained on him. He either avoided them or took them upon the flat of his shoulders or against the curtain of his arms as he wrapped them about his head.

Even so those blows rocked and shook him, battered him from side to side, stumbling and floundering. But he worked away from the wall of the cabin, where Runnell was trying to trap him. Luke managed to get into the clear, where he kept circling and weaving until strength began to come back into his legs and his head cleared.

Runnell was ferociously anxious to finish his man, to get another clean shot at him and, as Luke made no effort to hit back, Runnell forgot all defense or caution. He kept after Luke, swinging and smashing savagely.

Luke side-stepped once more, set himself and let one go, aiming for the center of Runnell's body as Runnell once more came rushing in. Luke was still lacking his full strength, but even so he got plenty behind that punch. Adding to the effect was the fact that Runnell was charging in. The punch landed solidly and Luke felt Runnell's stomach muscles give and cave under his knuckles and knew in that instant that he had hurt Runnell, hurt him bad. Nothing took it out of a man like an unexpected blow to the solar plexus. And the punch had caught Runnell with his belly muscles lax.

Bart Runnell gasped, a deep, thick, shuddering sound. He stopped his headlong charge, weaved, began to back up. Luke went after him, winging both fists. He felt his knuckles bite hard against Runnell's face and knew a ferocious pleasure at the impact. He smashed his right in and found Runnell's jaw, though a little high. Yet it was Runnell now who began to stumble and flounder.

Luke's strength was running stronger with every move. That was one thing about a smash to the jaw or face. Though such a blow might daze and stun for a moment, the effects wore off faster than from body punishment. A beating about the body stayed with a man, draining his strength, taking it out of him for a long, long time. And Runnell was still trying to fight off the effects of that solar-plexus wallop.

Luke gave him no time or chance. Remorseless as a wolf, he kept after his man. He jolted and shook and cut him up about the face. Then, as this punishment forced Runnell's guard up, Luke ripped another right hand to Runnell's softened, quivering midriff. This time Runnell's belly muscles really caved.

He groaned and bent forward and Luke brought one up savagely to meet Runnell's sagging jaw, and he found it, fairly. Runnell dropped, and stayed down.

Luke moved back, swaying a little. It seemed that lights were dancing before his eyes. He scrubbed the back of a hand across them, but still the light persisted. Then he realized that it was the light shining from the open door of the Leslie cabin. He had dropped Bart Runnell full in the middle of that outpour of yellow radiance.

He saw Dale Leslie, her face white and working, saw her dart out and drop on her knees beside Bart Runnell. Her white face lifted and her eyes blazed at Luke.

'You crude, ruthless barbarian!' she lashed. 'All you know, it seems, is to beat men down with your fists. I'll hate you for this! Forever and ever I'll hate you!'

'I wish,' mumbled Luke, 'I wish he was— more worthy of you. For there will be things come to light, I'm afraid—things—'

He broke off, scrubbed a hand across his face again, and this time there was something almost pathetically weary in the gesture. Then he stumbled off into the night.

Dale Leslie called to her brother. 'Dick— please! Give me a hand with Bart! He's hurt— bleeding. Hurry, Dick!'

Dick Leslie did not hurry. He came out of the cabin almost leisurely, a bucket of water in his hand. He slopped a copious part of the contents on Runnell's head and face—did it almost contemptuously. Runnell groaned, rolled over.

'We've got to get him into the house,' panted the distraught girl. 'He's hurt!'

'Not too bad,' observed Dick dryly. 'Another shot of water will do the trick.'

He spilled the balance of the pail's contents on the prostrate Runnell, who jerked to his hands and knees, mumbling a thick curse.

Dale Leslie gave of her slim strength to aid Runnell to his feet. 'Bart!' she cried. 'Let me help!'

Runnell's answer was to push her aside, pull free of her anxious hands and go lurching away into the dark.

CHAPTER SIX

NIGHT THUNDER

Steel was going down with ever-increasing speed. Johnny Megarry and the grade gang, no longer having to hold the entire job together, were out in front, slashing new, raw roadbed from the virgin earth. This was good roadbed construction country. The grade was very gradual, well under an average of one per cent, for the valley of the Castle River was a lazy one. Earth was sandy and easy to move along this particular stretch. The Fresno scrapers brought it up from either side of the right of way and the pick-and-shovel men smoothed and squared it to the grade stakes.

Right at their heels came Joe Keller and his steel gang, setting ties, laying steel, tying rails together with fishplates and bolts, lining up, gauging, driving spikes. The clatter and drive of industry echoed across the valley and up the slopes of the lonely, sage-clad hills on either side.

As fast as the steel crept out, the old Union Foundry engine clattered and clanked along it, pushing up still more loads of ties and steel and other supplies. Here, as Luke had foreseen, was where the old engine would more than earn its keep. The Simcoe was free for other more needful business on the run from Cold Creek to Garnet. Here Casey O'Keefe and the Union Foundry would see to it that the gangs would no longer have to wait for supplies when they were needed.

The word had gone out about Luke's promotion and the men seemed to approve heartily. Yet none spoke of it to him as he moved up and down along the job. For one thing, there was a bleakness about him, a remoteness of spirit which discouraged any talk beyond that necessary to the job. Even Johnny Megarry and Joe Keller were guided by the signs. And while all noted the bruised and swollen condition of Luke's mouth, men kept conjecture to themselves. Thus the lone wolf was more alone than ever before in his life.

During the noon hour Dick Leslie came down from up valley. He said to Luke, 'My bridge gang have just completed Number One. I'd like you to look it over if you will, Luke, and pass on it. I'm sure it will do, but you may have a couple of final suggestions.'

'Sure, Dick,' nodded Luke. 'Of course.'

The bridge lay a little more than half a mile beyond the end of steel. Up to here the right of way had run west of Castle River. But at Number One the river angled in and pinched up against the end of a low ridge which came in from the west and broke directly off above the river in a sheer sprung shoulder of rock. Keeping to the west of the river would have necessitated a lot of slow, costly excavating under the face of the bluffs, drill and powder work through solid, stubborn rock. It was cheaper to bridge here and go on up the long, smooth sweep of the valley to the east of the river. Cheaper and much, much faster.

Dick Leslie and his bridge gang had done a good job. Number One was soundly engineered, soundly constructed. Luke's opinion was a quiet, 'Very well done, Dick. A damn fine job. Pass that word on to your boys.'

Dick flushed with pleasure and said, 'Something else that won't please you, Luke.

120

Come on and I'll show you.'

Dick led the way on up the valley along the line of survey, with grade stakes marking the way. Then, abruptly, there were no more stakes. Dick said, 'From here on along, for a good three-quarters of a mile, someone has pulled up and thrown away all our survey and grade stakes. Who could it have been, I wonder? Maybe a wandering band of Shoshone Indians, messing up things just out of pure devilment and cussedness?'

Luke got out his pipe and studied the country as he smoked. The valley ran on and on to the south, swinging in great, lazy curves. On either side the low hills sloped up with their wilderness of everlasting sage, silent and masking. A vast and lonely land, this, with gulches swinging down from either hand, feeding out into the valley. A thousand ways in which vandals could creep down out of the sage, do their mischief and be gone again, without leaving trace or trail of where they had come from or where they had gone.

Luke shook his head. 'I don't believe Shoshones had anything to do with it, Dick. They're not a troublesome sort.'

'Of course there's no permanent damage done,' said Dick, 'except a waste of time. I've got all my figures and it won't take too long to set new stakes. Yet, at this stage of the game we can't afford time to be doing the most trivial jobs twice.'

'That's definitely right,' Luke nodded. 'We can't. So there will be steps taken to guard against such things in the future.'

Silently they headed back to the job. In this silence lay a growing strain. Abruptly Dick Leslie dropped a hand on Luke's arm and stopped him.

'Luke,' he said, 'I'm sorry about last night. But not over the fact that you gave Bart Runnell a damned good beating. That's something he's been asking for for a long time, and I was tickled to see him get it. I just want you to know that it hasn't changed my feelings toward you, except to make me like you better than ever. Dale—well, she was pretty upset. And she said things she'll probably change her mind about given time. She's pretty new to construction-camp conditions, and—well—'

'Sure,' said Luke quietly. 'I understand. I don't blame her for feeling as she does. She has certain ideas on dignity and human behavior which are quite correct. And a knock-down, drag-out brawl is never a pretty spectacle in any woman's eyes. No, I don't blame her in the slightest. So don't you.'

'You're decent as hell,' said Dick gruffly. Then in a burst of boyish candor he added, 'I can't understand what Dale sees in Bart Runnell. Oh, I'll admit when we first came out here Runnell seemed like a pretty good egg. But then of course he was top dog and everything was going his way. But of late there have been a lot of things crop up to push him around; and under the pressure he doesn't shape up too well. In fact, all of a sudden, I just can't stand the sight of him any more. Luke, that guy is crooked! Just how or where, I can't say for sure. But down underneath I'm dead certain of it.'

'He's a big, handsome devil,' said Luke. 'That always counts a lot in a woman's eyes. Yet there must be something decent about the man, that you and I can't see, Dick. While your sister can. For she is much too fine to be taken in by a complete rascal.'

'I'm not so sure about that,' grumbled Dick. 'Often it's the best women who can be the biggest fools in a case like that. Maybe if I could persuade Dale to go away for a while—'

Luke shook his head. 'That wouldn't do a lick of good. Best thing is to keep her right here in Cold Creek with you. For if Runnell is a complete crook, as you and I may figure he is, trust your sister to be smart enough to realize it. No problem was ever solved by running away from it.'

At the end of the day Luke climbed on a flat with the rest of the men and rode back to Cold Creek behind Casey O'Keefe and the old Union Foundry engine. The wind of movement pulled and tugged, brushing cool and sweet past a man's face. On it was the pungent breath of sage and juniper and the subtle, haunting, dry-sweet fragrance of some far distant cedar slope.

It was, thought Luke, a good way for a man to live and work. He felt a real kinship for the weary, sweaty and dirt-stained men about him. From job to job the country over, they drifted. They had stuck pick and shovel into the earth of a dozen different states. Always they were out in front, where things were opening up. Their sweat and toil, their brawn and endurance spanned rivers, crossed deserts, leveled mountains. They carved out the steel trails over which other men would travel in ease and comfort. And Luke wondered if those men and their women surrounded with luxury would ever give a thought to these men who made such luxury possible.

They wouldn't, of course, not many of them. But that didn't matter. These rough, tough, horny-handed men didn't need that comfort. For they were rich with an inner satisfaction, the satisfaction and pride of achievement. They built, they conquered. Other men only used. Nobody could take that satisfaction away from them.

After supper Luke went over to see John Guthrie and found the General Superintendent hard at work over a multitude of problems of supply and construction. Guthrie pushed a mass of papers aside, leaned back in his chair and stoked his pipe. He eyed Luke shrewdly, a twinkle in his eye.

'Been hearing things, I have,' he said. 'I'm

124

not asking a single question, Luke. But I understand you gave him a real whipping, and I'm glad. Sit down. I can see you've got other troubles on your mind.'

Luke told of the missing grade and survey stakes. 'We can expect more of that petty-larceny stuff—and probably worse, John. We'll be smart to realize right now that anything can happen before we put steel into Castle Mountain. I think it might be a good idea if we set about locating two or three men, riders preferably, who know this country, or at least know how to get around through this kind of country. Men who can read signs and follow trails, and men who can use a gun, if necessary. We should have half a dozen guns handy; rifles, along with ammunition. And some riding stock, several horses and saddles. What are the chances?'

Guthrie nodded. 'I've got to go to Garnet tomorrow on some other business. I'll take care of that if you really feel we need such things.'

'We'll need them. Something tells me this is going to be a knock-down and drag-out fight before it's finished. We know now that certain elements are out to make us miss that deadline and lose the subsidy. We'd be fools not to take precautions.'

'You've produced enough evidence to show that Jack Fargo has such ideas, Luke. You said—elements. Does that mean you suspect

125

similar intentions—from other sources?' Luke shrugged grimly. 'Call it a hunch, John. But I've a feeling this opposition goes a lot deeper than shows on the surface. Of one thing we can be fairly sure, the closer we come to putting the job over, the more open and tougher the opposition is going to be. So I believe we should be set for all eventualities.'

'I'll get you what you want,' promised Guthrie.

Luke moved slowly across town toward the boardinghouse. He was tired and would have welcomed sleep. Yet there was a nagging restlessness all through him. It was something that had been with him for days, now, and he had quit trying to kid himself as to the cause.

Dale Leslie.

It seemed that a picture of her was before him all the time. Not always the same picture. Mostly he tried to remember her as she had been the one time she seemed nearest to him—the night when she sat with him and Dick at the supper table, with the lamplight picking out the lights in her hair and laying soft shadows about her throat . . .

But it was hard to hang on to that picture because of another which kept thrusting at him—the picture of how she had looked at him and the things she had said as she knelt beside Bart Runnell and supported Runnell's head in her arms.

The sound of the bullet which flicked past

Luke's face jerked him back to realities like the crash of mountains falling down. The report came, round and hollow, from the blot of darkness before a small building. Instinct, not thinking, made Luke whirl and race toward the spot, low and driving.

Thinking would have called it a fool's play, but instinct made it the right one. Perhaps the man behind the treacherous shot figured Luke had a gun and was closing in for a direct shoot-out. At any rate, the fellow lost his nerve and ran for it. And when Luke reached the building he found nothing except the smell of powder smoke on the night air.

Little fires were running through Luke, thin and sharp and hot, calling for further pursuit. But Luke pulled himself up with a jerk of cold reason. He was unarmed and, though he had bluffed the gunman once, he might not be so lucky a second time. The sane thing to do was get out of there, fast!

Luke dodged over to another building, keeping close to it in the shelter of its massed shadow. Further along the street, aroused by the shot, men were calling back and forth, wondering. Luke kept moving swiftly on to Ma Megarry's place.

Johnny Megarry stood just outside the door, looking and listening. 'I thought I heard a shot,' he said.

There was no percentage in alarming Johnny to no end, so Luke answered, 'Was that what it was? I heard something, but didn't pay it much attention. Well, it's got the makings of a wild town and—'

Luke broke off abruptly as the hard, flat thud of commission reached them shaking the walls around them and laying a distinct push in the air, kept from being violent only by distance. Far down the valley there was a long, grumbling roll of echoes.

Johnny Megarry gulped. 'Now what could that be?'

Luke had whirled, his head high, his nostrils dilating almost as though he was keening the air. 'We keep no powder out at the end of construction,' he rapped harshly. 'And freighters that haul powder to the mines at Castle Mountain don't roll at night. It leaves only one answer, Johnny. Our bridge— Number One. They've blown our bridge!'

'Our bridge!' blurted Johnny. 'Now they wouldn't dare do that. Who—?'

Luke whirled back, grabbing the dazed Johnny by the arm. 'They'll dare anything, as we'll soon find out before we're done with this job. It's been crawling in me, the hunch of something like this taking place. Get Casey O'Keefe, Johnny. Tell him to get the old engine ready to roll. Hurry!'

Then Luke was gone, racing upstairs to his room. He didn't pause to scratch a light. By feel alone he located his old gripsack under the bed, opened and emptied it onto the spread. He found his holstered gun and belt, thumbed cartridges from belt loops, loaded the weapon, shoved it down inside the waistband of his jeans. Grabbing his short, fleece-lined coat, he sped down to the street.

Men were astir all over town, wondering about that mysterious blast. Several of them yelled questions at Luke as he raced along the street, but he paid no attention. Casey O'Keefe and his fireman were already at work on the Union Foundry engine. The regular work flats were still coupled to it and now men began climbing up on them, Johnny Megarry, Joe Keller and John Guthrie among others.

'Make it fast, Casey!' yelled Luke.

'Fast as I can, boy,' was Casey's answer. 'We'll roll as soon as I've enough steam to turn a wheel.'

'Look!' called Johnny Megarry. 'There's fire out there, too!'

Sure enough, across the night an angry glare was lifting, down along the Castle River Valley. Men watched the glare, their faces bleak and tight.

Through the gloom came another figure, running, a slim figure in gingham, hatless, coatless. It was Dale Leslie. Luke jumped down off the flatcar and caught her by the arm.

'Dale! Miss Leslie—what is it? This is no place for you. I thought Dick might show up—but not you.'

He could feel her trembling. 'That—that's

just it,' she panted, her voice small and ready to break. 'Dick—isn't here. He's—out there, where that blast was. He went out in a buckboard to get his theodolite, one of his surveying instruments. He'd left it there, forgot it when he came in from work. Now-that blast—and Dick—out there. I've got to get out there. You understand, don't you? Dick might be—hurt.'

Luke did not argue. He caught her by the elbows, tossed her on the flat and jumped up beside her, just as Casey O'Keefe yelled, 'Grab hold, everybody! We roll—!'

At first progress was maddeningly slow, for the steam pressure was so low the old engine made heavy work of it, but Casey and his fireman worked feverishly and soon the firebox rumbled and roared and the steam gauge climbed and with it the punch and speed of the old engine. They scudded swiftly and the night air, thin and cold, whistled and whipped along the flatcars.

Luke was abruptly conscious that the distraught girl beside him was shivering. He stripped off his fleece-lined coat and put it about her shoulders. 'Climb into that,' he ordered.

She didn't argue or protest, even when Luke buttoned it up under her chin. She was like a bewildered, frightened child. And when, with the increasing speed the cars began to lurch and sway, Luke put out a steadying arm that half encircled her, she still made no protest, just sitting there, hunched and silent.

The glare lifted higher and when they finally came rolling up to the blaze Luke saw that it was caused by a big stack of cross ties that had been piled ready to the needs of the steel gang. Luke was off the car before it stopped rolling. He ordered, 'Wait right there, Dale. If Dick is around here, we'll find him.'

But the girl wouldn't wait. She jumped down and ran on into the night, calling, 'Dick! Dick—!'

It seemed incredible that her call should bring an answer, but it did. Stumbling and weaving a trifle on his feet, Dick Leslie came moving into the glare of light from the burning ties, where he was fairly enveloped by his flying sister.

'Sis!' mumbled the young engineer, 'Sis! How did you get here? How did you guess—?'

'You're hurt, Dick!' wailed the girl. 'You're shaking!'

'I'm shook up, all right,' admitted Dick. 'But nothing worse. Easy, now. I'm all right.'

With his sister quieted, Dick told his story, looking at Luke across her shoulder. 'I drove out along the freight road until I was opposite Number One. I left the team and buckboard there and hiked in across the flat. All of a sudden the whole world blew up in my face. I had no warning. The blast picked me clear off the ground, knocked me end over end. It must

131

have knocked me out for a time. Anyhow, when I finally got to realize where I was and got back on my feet, here came the engine headlight, ramming along through the night. But I'm all right. Nothing busted that I know of. I just feel kind of—top-heavy!'

Dick wobbled a little as he spoke and Luke said, 'Sit down here and take it easy, kid. Keep him here, Miss Leslie.'

John Guthrie, Joe Keller and Johnny Megarry were already heading out for Number One. Luke hurried after them. John Guthrie said bitterly, 'They poured kerosene over those ties before touching off the blaze, the damned, sneaking vandals!'

Which was true enough. The greasy smoke from the ties was rank with the stench of kerosene. The night was full of the smell of charred and smoldering wood. And now, as they came up to where Number One bridge had stood, they smelled the sweetish odor of blasting powder smoke.

All about them were chunks of timber, splintered and twisted, acrid and stinking with smoke, with sullen red eyes of smoldering coals staring through the gloom. And where Number One had stood, staunch and sturdy as Luke Fenimore had last seen it, was now only a black and empty gap.

'They used enough powder to move a mountain, let alone a bridge,' said Luke. 'No wonder the blast shook the town.'

John Guthrie was silent for a long moment, staring at destruction. 'I see what you meant, Luke,' he said curtly. 'What you asked me for tonight will be in Cold Creek by this time tomorrow.'

Johnny Megarry, opening and closing his big hands in helpless anger, growled, 'We start cleaning up this mess tonight, if you say so, Luke.'

'No, that won't be necessary, Johnny.' Then Luke added softly, as though to himself, 'They made a big mistake. They've shown their hands just a little too soon.'

After a search they found Dick Leslie's theodolite several yards back from the bridge. The concussion had knocked it down, but as far as Luke could tell by the light of a match, the instrument had not been damaged. He carried it back to the cars, where Casey O'Keefe and his fireman had not been idle. With a couple of crowbars they had been at work tearing apart the pile of burning cross ties and as a consequence had saved quite a number.

Luke turned to Johnny Megarry. 'How about driving Dick's buckboard back to town, big feller? The quicker we get Dick home and into the blankets, the better it will be for him.'

Johnny said simply, 'You took the words out of my mouth, Luke. I was going to suggest that. Be seeing you.'

Johnny went off into the night and the rest

133

of them got back onto the cars. With a full head of steam in the old engine now, Casey O'Keefe rolled them swiftly back to Cold Creek. Luke took Dick Leslie's arm and walked with him and his sister up to their cabin, where he said, 'Take a hot bath, kid, and then hit the blankets. Don't worry about getting on the job too soon tomorrow. Catch a ride out to the job with Casey later in the day. A good sleep should fix you up all right.'

Dick said, 'But the bridge. This will put us way behind. I got to get at that bridge right away.'

'The mess will have to be cleaned up before you can start rebuilding,' Luke told him. 'I'll get some of the men at that, first thing tomorrow. You take it easy. Be seeing you.'

Now it was Dale Leslie, taking off Luke's coat, holding it out to him. She had steadied and quieted and was much her old self again. 'Thank you,' she said gravely. 'Thank you— very much. You've been kind. Good night!'

*   *   *

Luke's advice to Dick Leslie about a hot bath and bed he might very well have taken with advantage himself, for there was weariness dragging at his very bones. Not so much a physical weariness as fatigue that comes from burned-out nervous energy and bottled-up emotion. But the old restlessness was eating at

134

him, too, so, instead of heading for Ma Megarry's place, he went across town and out to the rolling, sage-covered hills beyond. Well up on the slope of one of them, with the spice of sage breath all about him, he hunkered down on his heels, got out his pipe and stared across the ragged blur of the stilling town with its uneven beading of lights.

In a way he felt relieved. All along he had known something would happen, a blow somewhere. It was, as he had told John Guthrie, more than an instinct, a hunch. Logical thinking had all along pointed to the same thing. Yes, this had been in the books from the first.

The waiting for the blow to fall had been tough, as waiting always was. Now it had happened and, coldly measured, it was not as bad as it might have been. Something of this sort at a later date would have hurt much worse than now. Not but what something else as bad, or worse, could not be expected in the future. But in the future they would be better prepared—they would be on guard. At last the cards were beginning to fall openly, where a man could read them. Jack Fargo, it seemed, was beginning to push his bets.

It's always a relief, thought Luke, when you know you have a fight ahead of you, to have the fight start, to be done with waiting. When you had your adversary directly in front of you you could measure him, test him, plan your strategy and go after him. That was how things were shaping up now.

By the time Luke's pipe sucked dry and cold, he was once more relaxed and easy. Only, far back in his eyes lay a steady, settled hardness. It was the look of a man who, having committed himself to a difficult task, would be as ruthless, as unyielding and as savage as need be to finish it. The lone wolf was definitely alone, but prowling.

Luke knocked the dottle from his pipe on his boot heel, straightened up and went back down the low slope to town. But now he watched every shadow, laying the fine edge of alert senses across them as he passed. He wasn't forgetting that sneak shot.

Glancing in at the Big Sage saloon he saw Jack Fargo. The freighter was at a card table, playing draw poker with four mule skinners. Sudden and harsh decision gleamed in Luke's eyes and he went into the place quietly, drifting around to come up in back of Fargo's chair. He stood there, watching Fargo drag in two sizable pots in quick succession.

One of the skinners said irritably, 'Damn you Jack—you got the luck of the devil. I don't know why you go to the bother of paying me wages. You get it all back again with the cards. Well, this is a big plenty for me, if I expect to go on eating till next payday.'

The other three skinners seemed to have had enough also, for they pushed back their chairs and followed the speaker to the bar. Fargo, counting and pocketing his winnings, called casually to the bartender, 'Give the boys what they want, Rip. It's on me.'

His money pocketed, Fargo stood up and turned, and saw Luke for the first time. Fargo was startled, definitely so, and Luke saw the pupils of his eyes dilate like those of a wary animal. But only for a split second. Then an inscrutable curtain seemed to lower across them. Luke saw anger also lift its head, but that too was quickly subdued.

This man Fargo was an actor, for he even managed what might have passed as a friendly smile. But the heartiness in his voice was plainly false as he said, 'Hello, Fenimore. How are things? You railroad fellows seem to be making pretty good time these days. If your luck holds you shouldn't have too much trouble beating that subsidy deadline.'

A few days ago Luke might have fenced with him. But not tonight. Not after that sneak shot from the dark. Not after the dynamiting of Number One bridge.

'We figure to make it,' Luke came back curtly. 'But not on luck. We're not counting on luck. We're going to depend on hard work, straight thinking and tough action. We expect to be just three times as tough as the damned lice who are trying to hold us up. That means you, Fargo, with your blocking us off from the Grasshopper steel we were after, and your

137

attempt to pull the same kind of deal on the White Queen steel at Corinth. We figure to make it even if you did blow our Number One bridge tonight and burn a stack of our cross ties. Yeah, we figure to make it in spite of all that.'

Again was Fargo definitely shaken. Again Luke saw the eyes of the teamster boss dilate in that startled way. And now the false front of friendliness disappeared. A thread of bluster came into Fargo's tone. 'You must have gone loco,' he growled. 'I don't know what you're talking about. Why, I ain't been out of this place all evening.'

'Perhaps not,' shot back Luke, 'but how about some of your pet coyotes, like Bole Ives and Cob Ogard? No—no, Fargo. You're not fooling anybody. For a time I was afraid you had enough in you to play it big, to think a little faster. But you're not that big. You're just like any other small-time crook. When you're cornered you fall back on a lie.'

'Just a minute, just a minute!' blustered Fargo. 'There's a word I don't like and don't take from any—'

'I gave it to you once, I give it to you again,' cut in Luke. 'Crook, was what I said. I say it again. You're a crook, Fargo—a small-time one. And now, if you want to make anything of it, why, there you are and here I am. And there's no time like the present. Go ahead—cut your wolf loose!'

Their eyes met and locked and Jack Fargo's were the first to waver. Luke Fenimore laughed. 'I see it won't be now. Well, that's all right. Any time, Fargo—any time. But right now I want to say to you that the gloves are off from here on in. Word you can take to heart yourself and that you can pass along to Bole Ives, Cob Ogard or anyone else you got lined up to do your dirty work for you. You're not near as smart as you think, or half as tough. Neither are they. And something else. Next time one of you takes a shot at me in the dark, you better make it good, or it will be the last time. So, there it is, Fargo. Chew on it. Remember, from here on in we play it rough!'

Luke turned and went out, leaving Fargo standing there. Luke had made no attempt to keep his tone pitched low, so his words had carried to every man in the room. He felt their eyes on him now as he walked out, his well-packed shoulders loose and easy. The four mule skinners looked at each other, looked at Fargo. When Luke had disappeared, every man in the saloon looked at Jack Fargo, watching and waiting in silence.

They were measuring him, and Fargo knew it. They were measuring and weighing and judging. They were remembering that the man who had just called Fargo was the same who had whipped Cob Ogard to a stunned and bleeding heap. Some of them knew that Luke Fenimore had faced three of Jack Fargo's roughest, toughest mule skinners in the caboose at Kicking Horse water tower atop Rockaway Pass, thrown them off the train. And a few knew that Luke Fenimore had soundly beaten Bart Runnell a few nights previous. A fighting man, Luke Fenimore, who had now called Jack Fargo, called him cold. And Fargo had backed down. This was what the men in the Big Sage were thinking. And Fargo knew it.

Fargo also knew how men like these judged other men. There was no room in their minds for intricate reasonings. There was nothing complicated about the work they did or the lives they led. The simple fundamentals were good enough for them and that was the way their minds ran. Physical courage was almost a fetish with them. A man had it or he didn't. And if he lacked it, their judgment could be quick and final and brutal. Now they were watching him, Jack Fargo, and wondering.

There were black currents seething in Jack Fargo, and only those who knew him fully knew the fight he was putting on to keep such currents under control. The bartender was one of these and there was almost a grudging admiration in his eyes as he watched Fargo make his fight, and win it. Fargo shrugged, stepped up to the bar, spilled some money on it. A faint smile pulled at his lips.

'He had a gun,' Fargo said. 'A gun stuck in his belt, covered by the flap of his coat. Only a damn fool bets against a hand as pat as that one was. Because'—and here his bony face creased with an expression that was thin and malignant—'there's always another hand coming up. Step up, boys, and name your pleasure!'

CHAPTER SEVEN

DAYS ON ACCOUNT

When the crews hit the job the next morning—and got a good look at the damage, they were fighting mad. Luke Fenimore let them blow off steam for a few minutes, then said, 'Snow on the other side of the mountain, boys. It'll be all the same a hundred years from now. Let's get going.'

Casey O'Keefe rolled another flat of ties up from Cold Creek and the job went ahead. Despite Luke's advice of the night before, Dick Leslie was on the job with the rest of them, a little pale, but otherwise as good as ever. Luke sent him and his survey crew up ahead to reset grade stakes that had been torn up, and pitched into the bridge-repair job himself.

It was a tough, dirty chore. No man likes to rebuild a job, but Luke gave the men little time to think. He got right down into the middle of the mess with them and began moving torn and blast-blackened timbers. The work went on in a grim and bitter silence.

Luke wondered how many of the men were thinking as he was; that the deadline, and the subsidy riding on it, had drawn a little further away. Though he admitted it to no one, he knew that that subsidy and deadline were beginning to haunt him. It was going to be close, so very close. It might thin down to an hour or less. Even a hundred yards, one way or another, could be vital.

Maybe the men were thinking of these possibilities. At any rate they worked with a dogged, bitter intentness; and by quitting time that night fresh timbers were being bolted into place and the bridge was beginning to take shape again.

Johnny Megarry's grade crew worked up to the river, then dragged their equipment across the trickling flow of water and went on from the other side. And the Union Foundry engine was riding steel to within a hundred yards of Number One when the weary crews stacked their tools at the end of the day.

When Casey O'Keefe rolled them back into Cold Creek, there was the Simcoe, panting gustily from its run in from Garnet. John Guthrie was there, supervising the unloading of half a dozen horses from a boxcar.

'Everything you asked for, Luke,' said Guthrie. 'Horses, riding gear, guns—

everything. But men like you asked for are something else again. I managed to locate just one man named Keno Udell. He preferred to ride his own horse in from Garnet and should show up some time tomorrow. From what I could find out, this Udell is as good as a dozen ordinary men when it comes to understanding the country and knowing how to read a trail.'

'Fair enough, John,' nodded Luke. 'A couple of those horses will get a workout tonight.'

'A jag of guarding, eh?'

'I'm taking Joe Keller with me.'

'Why not a couple of men from one of the crews?'

Luke shook his head. 'The men really put out today. They work a lot harder physically than Joe and I do.'

As Luke was on his way to the boardinghouse, Dick Leslie came hurrying to catch up and fall in step with him. 'Luke, what's to keep more devilment from hitting Number One again tonight?'

'Joe Keller and me,' answered Luke dryly. 'Plus a couple of Winchester rifles.'

Dick looked crestfallen. 'I was hoping to draw that chore myself,' he confessed.

Luke grinned. 'You had enough excitement last night to last you for awhile, Dick. I'm not letting you take any more risks.'

'If it is Dale's feelings you're worrying about, you needn't,' argued Dick. 'She was plenty scared last night, but this morning there was fire in her eyes. And she was especially nice to brother.'

'Lucky brother,' murmured Luke. 'Just the same I'll not have her worry about you again tonight. You stay home.'

With rifles across their saddles, Luke and Joe Keller rode out of town in the first gloom of night, following the right of way across the miles to Number One. Arriving there, they found a place where the sage pushed down from the west valley slope and settled there at their ease. They watched the dark swoop of the night build up, smelled the haunting breath of the wild wasteland, listened to its sounds. They watched the stars bud and brighten, they smoked and relaxed and talked.

Each had a backlog of construction-job recollections to recall, and in this manner they killed the early hours. But gradually they fell silent and cushioned the slow pace of the hours against the stream of their own more intimate thoughts. They pulled their coat collars about their ears and shed the chill of the night stoically. And they heard nothing, nor saw anything.

Midnight came and with it the first sound that was not of the natural land and night. Luke stood up, listening. 'Some kind of rig coming along the freight road, Joe.'

'Maybe,' said Joe reaching for his rifle, 'maybe we'll have some fun after all.'

Joe's suggestion seemed to gather point as

they heard the rig move up and stop opposite them. Then they were startled to hear Dick Leslie's voice lift in a hail. 'Luke—Joe! You fellows down there somewhere?'

'Right here, Dick,' Luke called back. 'What's wrong?'

'Not a thing. How'd you like some hot coffee? Come on, Sis, they're right below us. Here, give me that coffee jug. Watch your step!'

They came down through the dark sage, Dick carrying a thick pottery jug, wrapped in a blanket and filled with coffee. Dale had a big box of sandwiches. Luke said 'You two kids are crazy—but wonderful.'

The girl was silent, but Dick said, 'It was Dale's idea, mainly. Now if we can put a little fire together, so we can see what we're doing—'

Dick and Joe Keller got busy in a little clearing, and Luke, looking down at the silent girl beside him, murmured, 'I was right. I knew I had to be right. Behind the loveliness there is gentleness.'

Still silent, she moved a little apart from him. But Luke was content. Her very reticence was an admission of amity.

The coffee, kept hot by the thick pottery jug and the wrapping of blankets, steamed its fragrance, and from the sandwich box Dale Leslie produced some cups. They relaxed about the blaze, eating and drinking. Joe

145

Keller mumbled, his mouth full, 'Sure glad you folks came out. I had just been thinking of how good a cup of coffee and a bite would taste. This is the best grub I ever ate.'

Across the flames, Luke guardedly studied the expression on Dale Leslie's face. There was gravity there, but serenity also. It was as though she had finally settled in her own mind a decision difficult to arrive at. But once this was done, it seemed to have brought relief and emotional peace.

There was so much to this girl, thought Luke, such a vital aliveness, that her presence was always positive, even when she was silent. Her mere presence brought a man contentment.

Joe Keller reached for the coffee jug, to refill his cup. And then, out across the valley, a pencil of pale flame licked out and was gone again in a split second. The echo of the report bounced and skidded up the valley.

Joe Keller's reaching arm was smashed aside, as though some invisible hand had caught it and jerked it violently, so violently that it nearly flung him face down across the flames. In his lurching effort to prevent this, Joe upset the coffee jug on the fire and the bulk of the flames went out in a hiss of steam.

For a breath Luke Fenimore was frozen to immobility. Then he grabbed Joe and pulled him clear. And as he stamped the rest of the fire embers to blackness, he rapped harshly,

'Get Dale out of here, Dick—quick!'

Another slug came winging, smashing right at Luke's feet. Luke fumbled in the dark, found his rifle and raced off some twenty yards. There he picked up the winking gun flame of a third shot and levered three quick shots in reply. These served the purpose. They drew the next shot from the opposite dark, the slug whipping by a couple of yards above Luke's head. Luke gave it back, two more shots. It was, of course, utterly blind shooting, with not one chance in a thousand of hitting anything. But it served the purpose of making that treacherous skulker realize that this was far from being one-sided.

No further shooting came, but a fading yell echoed, taunting and harsh with the implication that there would be another time. After that silence.

Luke hurried back to where the fire had been, calling for Joe Keller.

'Right here, Luke,' answered Joe, his voice thin and tired. 'They gave me a bad arm. Busted clean as a pipestem. The dirty whelps! They might have hit Dale Leslie!'

'But they didn't,' came the girl's voice. 'They hit you—and that arm needs attention.'

Luke got an arm about Joe. 'Up the ridge to the buckboard, old-timer. Put plenty of weight on me.'

There was a blanket in the buckboard and Luke hung this on some sage. He made Joe squat down behind it and there, while Dick scratched one match after another for frugal light, Luke and Dale bandaged the arm as best they could with handkerchiefs.

'Now to town, as fast as you and Dale can get him there, Dick,' said Luke. 'Into the buckboard, Joe. These good folks will have you in a doctor's hands in jig time. I'll bring in your horse and other gear.'

As Dick Leslie gathered up the reins he said, 'Watch yourself, Luke. That yell, just now. I heard another like it, once before. He was drunk, on the prod and looking for a fight. Yeah, I heard him yell just like that, at another time.

'Who?'

'Cob Ogard!'

* * *

The job moved along. On hearing what had happened to Joe Keller, the men stared at the silent, mocking sage, cursed and took out their feelings in work. The bridge gang did tremendous labors and steel crossed the river for the first time, after which Casey O'Keefe rolled the old Union Foundry engine across, pushing up flats loaded with ties and steel. The bridge gang, finished with Number One, began moving timber and tools and equipment up to the site of Number Two. Luke put Johnny Megarry in charge of both the steel and the grade gangs.

'I'll work you down to skin and bone, big boy,' Luke told him.

Johnny flexed his big hands and said grimly, 'Could I get hold of the rat who did that to Joe Keller, there'd not even be skin and bone left of him. Don't worry about me, Luke.'

There was a little wrinkled gnome of an old-timer, named Flick Lee, who had been handling the reins of one of the Fresno-scraper teams. The pace of the job, plus age, was beginning to get the best of him. Luke drew him aside.

'New job for you, Flick, but with the same pay. Can you stay awake nights, and can you handle a Winchester?'

'I'm a night hawk by preference,' vowed Flick. 'And I've handled a Winchester plenty in my time.'

'Good! Starting tonight you guard Number One. Should anybody come prowling around who has no business there, shoot, and shoot for keeps.'

'I can do that, too,' said Flick Lee.

Late in the afternoon a rider came jogging in from the north. 'I'm Keno Udell,' he told Luke. 'Mr. Guthrie hired me. He said you'd tell me what to do.'

Keno Udell was small and restless, with the look of tough rawhide about him. He was alert as a wild animal. He seemed always to be looking and listening. His hand grip was firm,

149

his eyes steady.

Luke told him the setup, listed what had happened and said he expected more of the same. 'Chances are,' said Luke, 'that whoever is making this trouble for us has a camp somewhere out in the sage. They're not around town any more. Try and find that camp. Just keep scouting and see what trails you run across. Use your own judgment where to ride and look.'

Keno Udell nodded, then asked one short question. 'In case of trouble, just how far do I go?'

'Just as far as you have to. Anything, so we stop this trouble in its tracks. If it calls for powder smoke, spread your share of it. You'll be backed to a finish.'

'Keno!' said Udell, giving index to his nickname. 'That's all I wanted to know.'

As soon as the work train got back to town that night, Luke hurried up to the boardinghouse and went to Joe Keller's room. Joe, one arm and shoulder bandaged, lay in bed. Sitting on a chair beside the bunk was Dale Leslie.

Luke said, 'Whoa! Didn't mean to butt in.'

Joe grinned. 'It's all right. Dale just brought me something tasty for supper. Sometimes it pays to stop a slug, Luke.'

'Feeling pretty chipper, are you?'

'Well,' said Joe wryly, 'I wouldn't say I felt exactly ready to go out and knock a mountain down, but I'm what the doc would call resting reasonable comfortable. Give me a few days and I'll be out there to keep an eye on my gang.'

Luke looked at the girl. 'What's your opinion, Miss Leslie?'

'The doctor said he'll be right where he is for at least two weeks. I think he's right.'

'Then,' said Luke, 'that's orders, Joe. And you don't have to worry about your gang. Nobody needs to keep an eye on them. They're going full out.'

Dale Leslie stood up. 'I've got to be going. Dick will be wondering about his supper.'

Joe called after her, 'Thanks a heap, Miss Dale. You're swell.'

Then, as the door closed behind her, Joe looked at Luke and growled, 'She is swell. They don't come any finer than that girl. But just what she can see in a guy like Bart Runnell has got me whipped.'

Luke stepped to the window and looked out. He saw Dale Leslie angle across the street through the new dusk, heading for her cabin. And he saw a man step out of a doorway, speak to her and then go along with her. There was no mistaking that tall, square-shouldered figure. It was Bart Runnell.

Luke stood for some little time staring out of that window. Finally Joe Keller said, 'What the devil are you staring at? What's out there?'

Luke turned back; then, 'I was just

151

thinking.'

Joe, eying him keenly, said, 'Don't let the pressure of this job make an old man of you, Luke. No job is worth getting that kind of a look over it. Like it was twisting you up inside.'

Luke managed a mirthless grin. 'Good Lord! Am I that bad? The job was worth you getting a smashed flipper, wasn't it?'

Joe grunted. 'I might have busted it wrestling steel. Call it one of the hazards of the job.'

'So is my misery, I guess,' admitted Luke. 'But we sure aim to get even for that arm of yours, feller.' And Luke told Joe about Keno Udell. 'He locates that rat nest,' Luke ended, 'and we'll sure hold a house cleaning.'

Luke shaved, cleaned up and had his supper. After that he killed a full hour in his room, pacing up and down, sucking at his pipe, struggling with the problem gnawing at him. Finally, grim and determined, he slid his gun under his belt, donned hat and coat and went out, heading straight for the Leslie cabin. At his knock Dale Leslie opened the door.

'Dick isn't here,' she said. 'He's at the hotel, seeing Mr. Guthrie about something.'

'How about Runnell?' asked Luke. 'Is he here?'

Dale colored slightly, shaking her head.

'Fine!' said Luke. 'I was hoping to find you alone. There are some things you and I must talk about.'

152

She hesitated, nodded. 'Come in.'

Luke did not take the chair she indicated. He stood, facing her across the table. 'I'm afraid this won't improve the quality of our rather dubious friendship, Miss Leslie.' A faintly sardonic smile pulled at his lips, as though he was reviewing some inner joke on himself. He went on, 'Which is all right, too, for I've quit trying to kid myself about you and me. I had hoped I might win your better regard, but I see it's still Runnell and probably always will be. So that's that. After all, a man can hang on to a hope just so long, and then it goes sour on him.'

Several expressions had crossed Dale Leslie's face while Luke spoke. She had been still and reserved. Then she flushed. Now she was watching him with enigmatic eyes.

'I know I've got a lot of rough edges,' Luke continued. 'But I've come by them honestly. If I deal in fundamentals it's because I've had to in the work I've followed all my life. Which may all be beside the point, though it was something I had to get off my chest. The main thing I came to see you about is Runnell.'

She had been listening quietly, that strange, veiled look in her eyes. Now, however, a flash of spirit burned away that veil and she said curtly, 'I don't know why you should. It is definitely none of your business.'

'On the contrary,' Luke said grimly. 'Oh, it's nothing to do with your friendship for him. On

153

that angle you're quite right, it is none of my business. But there is something else. It has to do with the fact that Runnell is one of the enemies of the Desert & Central Railroad—one of the crowd trying to keep us from beating that deadline and winning the subsidy.'

'You're sure of that?' demanded Dale. 'You've proof of such an accusation—or is it just your enmity toward Bart that makes you say this?'

'My personal feelings have nothing to do with it,' Luke said. 'Should Runnell hate me to my dying day I'd probably stand up under the strain. I'm thinking about the moves already made against the job. Such as blowing up Number One bridge, a little trick that came very close to killing your brother Dick. And of a sneak shot from the dark which came even closer to killing Joe Keller. Those are facts beyond denial.'

'Facts—yes. But you have no grounds for saying Bart Runnell had anything to do with them.'

'Sometimes, Miss Leslie, it's possible to arrive at an answer by putting two and two together,' Luke said dryly. 'Let's start with the Grasshopper steel fiasco. John Guthrie sent Runnell after that steel. Who tipped Jack Fargo off so he could move in and tie up the steel before we could get it? Certainly John Guthrie didn't. But that's what happened. And did Runnell seem at all downcast over his failure the night he returned and stood in this very room and reported that failure in reply to your brother's question? He did not! Which Dick couldn't understand, and neither could I.'

'That still doesn't prove anything as serious as your charge against Bart,' retorted the girl.

'Very well. How about the mess the grade gang was in? Why didn't Runnell do something about that? It was his responsibility to straighten out that gang and get it moving again. To anyone who knew the first thing about construction gangs and what makes them behave the way they do, it was obvious that Bole Ives and Cob Ogard were the cause of all the trouble. Why didn't Runnell get rid of them? And again, why did he try to interfere and take their part when I moved to fire them? You must admit a pattern taking shape, Miss Leslie.'

Luke kept his glance boring at the girl and now her eyes wavered and little spots of color burned in her cheeks. 'It could have been Bart's resentment against you that made him obstruct,' she said. 'Have you ever thought of that?'

'He owed more allegiance to the success of the job than to his personal feelings,' Luke said bluntly. 'Something else. The night Curt Leffingwell fired him, Runnell made his threats—not against me, particularly, but against the railroad and its chances of reaching Castle Mountain ahead of the deadline. There

155

are so many things which add up to one logical answer. You must admit that.'

'And you must admit something which makes all your guesses seem farfetched,' put in Dale quickly. 'Bart Runnell is Henry Shard's nephew. Would he deliberately undermine his own uncle's interests?'

Luke shrugged. 'He might, to serve his own personal fortune. I gathered that Henry Shard was somewhat disappointed in his nephew. And while Shard admitted the relationship, just how much personal attachment exists is anybody's guess. If Jack Fargo made it worth his while to gum up the works, I don't think Runnell would hesitate a second in changing sides.'

'That is unfair,' charged Dale Leslie. 'The other evening Dick was angry at Bart for making charges against you behind your back. I wonder how he would feel now if he were here?'

'You might be surprised,' was Luke's terse reply. He made a little weary gesture with his hand. Then he brushed back his coat to show the butt of the gun he was carrying. 'I'm not packing this gun because I like the weight of it. But the other night, right here in town, somebody took a shot at me. That's the way this job is shaping up, Miss Leslie. Tough. Anything can happen. There are a lot of good men working on the job and they don't like the idea of bridges being dynamited and a popular boss like Joe Keller being wounded by a vandal rifle shot. If they should catch Bart Runnell mixed up in any such tricks, I can't guarantee his safety for you. You have your own reasons for being fond of Bart Runnell and if he gets hurt, that would hurt you. And— I don't want to see you hurt.'

Again she gnawed at a red underlip, her glance grave and quieting as she studied Luke. 'Just what would you have me do?' she asked finally.

'Two things,' Luke told her. 'In fairness to your brother Dick, whose whole heart and soul is dedicated to the success of this job ahead of us, don't discuss any future plans which Dick might mention to you with Bart Runnell. You owe that to Dick, if to no one else. Secondly, I'd suggest you do all you can to influence Runnell to get completely clear of Fargo and his gang and stay that way. Which is about all, I guess. Good night, Miss Leslie.'

After the door closed behind Luke, Dale Leslie stood right where she was for some time, shadowy-eyed and deeply thoughtful.

*   *   *

The grade from Cold Creek to Castle Mountain lifted steadily through a narrowing valley into canyon country where rock ledges shouldered up to block the way. Now the clank of sledge hammer on steel drill echoed across

157

the sage and at quickening intervals the rolling crash of dynamite blasts bludgeoned the far distances.

Luke Fenimore became increasingly aware of the pressure of time. That was the hell about time. It never quit moving, it never stood still. A man could neither stop it nor slow it nor hold it back by one remorseless clock tick. A man had to keep apace or ahead of it. Otherwise it caught him by the throat, strangling and overwhelming him.

As with all opposition, there was a peak, a high point. On this job it shaped up at a spot only six short miles below Castle Mountain. Here the valley which had become a canyon became a gorge and in this gorge the rock pushed in on either hand, not lofty, but stubborn and precipitous. Here, through a gap less than fifty feet wide the rare, but brutal flood waters of Castle River beat their way. Here would be the final bridge, Number Four. It could cross the river at an angle but had to be lofty enough to clear the highest flood water. It was a challenge to young Dick Leslie's engineering ability, and he faced the task soberly.

Another thing was decided upon. This was to move the quarters of the crew closer to construction. Rancheria Flat, which lay between bridges Three and Four, was selected. The buildings would be of tar paper and lath, which was quick, easy construction and would serve, now that the weather was growing steadily milder. One thing was starkly clear. Every ounce from every man would be needed from here on in.

Realizing this the men responded. They had conquered rock and tough going before, and wasted no time now. Drills crashed into virgin stone. Powder was set, fused and capped and then tore a path with gargantuan strength. The men were back at the shattered debris before the dust and powder fumes had barely cleared. They moved rock and earth and went forward. And they laid steel, always more steel.

Came the day when Casey O'Keefe nursed the old Union Foundry rig across bridge Number Two and steel moved on toward Number Three. Now Flick Lee guarded Number Two while another old-timer was put in Flick's place at Number One. Keno Udell rode the sage, coming and going at odd moments, a restless little man who watched and listened and seemed to be eternally sniffing the air like an alert animal.

Tough as he was physically, Luke began to show the strain. His eyes grew shadowed, deep-sunken, and his face leaned to a set and stubborn mask. He had plenty on his mind. Along with all the multitudinous details of the job itself he found himself waiting and wondering when and where Jack Fargo and his men would strike again. He saw nothing of Fargo, who seemed to have dropped from

159

sight, but Fargo's freight wagons were always rolling, to and from Castle Mountain.

Luke wondered about that. Fargo held some powerful cards in the freighting setup. If he were to stop his wagons rolling it would be a stiff blow to the mineowners. The fact that he did not meant one of two things. Either he was sure the deadline could no longer be beaten, or he had some other plan for causing trouble and was merely waiting the time and place.

Steel moved on. Tragedy struck. A powder man grew careless, cut a fuse short, was slow in getting away. A chunk of rock, hurtling from the blast like a cannon shell, caught him. They buried him in the evening, when the shadows were blue and still. They set a primitive headstone and went on.

Death tried again, barely missing. They had blown off the point of a rock shoulder and were bringing the broken rubble down to grade level. A slab of rock weighing tons was poised more delicately than any of them knew. A man with a pick went to work below it and the thudding pick tipped that delicate balance.

Luke Fenimore was standing a few yards away. He saw the slab stir and begin to topple. The man beneath it, engrossed in his work, had no inkling. There was no time to shout or warn, only to act. Luke raced in and dove. His driving shoulder lifted the man and sent him sprawling to one side. Luke fell half across him and the slab, thudding ponderously down, caught Luke's boot heel with such stunning force as to leave his foot numbed for an hour after.

The man got up, stared, went momentarily white. Then he grinned, wiped the sweat from his face and put out his hand. 'Thanks, boss,' he said and went back to work.

Twice the Big Three—Curt Leffingwell, Frank Ames and Henry Shard—drove down from Castle Mountain to look over the job. They listened to Luke's report on the blowing of Number One bridge in grim-faced silence. When Luke told of his preparations against warding off any more disastrous sabotage, they nodded quick approval.

'Pull no punches, Luke,' growled Leffingwell. 'Kill if you have to. We'll back you to the limit. You're laying steel faster than I ever thought possible. The way things are moving I'm beginning to have real hope.'

Luke nodded. 'Any suggestions or orders?'

'Not a thing,' said Frank Ames quickly. 'We'd be fools to make a suggestion, even if we thought one were needed, which we don't. You have your schedule and your plans worked out. Stay with them. If we come browsing around to look things over, it is merely because this thing has us by the throat, Luke, the same as it has you and Guthrie and every other man on the job. Don't pay any attention to us. This thing is in your hands, not ours.'

Steel moved on, always on. It crossed

Number Three bridge and reached Rancheria Flat. John Guthrie had the new quarters ready for the men and Casey O'Keefe hauled up all the bedding and other belongings along with the supplies for the grub shacks. A single small shanty stood off to one side and Luke wondered why Guthrie had built that one, until one day he glimpsed Dale Leslie busily engaged in sweeping it out.

Luke got hold of Dick Leslie and said, 'You shouldn't have let your sister come up here to Rancheria Flat. She's entitled to better quarters than those, Dick.'

Dick shrugged: 'I tried to get her to stay in Cold Creek, but I might as well have saved my breath. She went over my head to Mr. Guthrie and wangled him into building that shanty for her. Maybe if you tried, Luke, you might convince her.'

Luke tried it. She was outside, industriously hoeing weeds when Luke went over. She straightened up, tossed back a lock of hair that had fallen over one eye, and said briskly, 'If you've come to scold, I won't listen to you. Otherwise—' and here a glimmer of a smile touched her lips '—I'll be glad to show you how comfortable my little home is.'

Luke was startled. This girl was different. No longer did she look at him as though from a distance, cold and aloof. There was a hint of real friendliness such as she had never shown him before.

Luke said gravely, 'I won't scold.'

She led the way inside and here indeed was comfort and cheer. Here was color and warmth through the magic of a woman's touch. Luke said, 'You win. But I still say it's bound to be lonely for you, with the nearest of your sex at Cold Creek, or Castle Mountain, which is still out ahead.'

'You men!' she scoffed. 'You sound just like Dick when you talk that way. You like to think that all women are soft, puny things who must be surrounded with luxuries to be content. Which shows how little you know about us. Perhaps we can't drag a fellow workman from sure death beneath a falling rock, but at least we can endure a little hardship in the interest of the job. How could I be lonely when all day long the thunder of blasts rolls and rumbles and the steel goes down and Casey O'Keefe rattles by in his old engine and blows his whistle at me? No, I'm anything but lonely.'

'There'll probably be ants and scorpions and wood rats to plague you,' Luke warned, smiling.

'There could be far more unpleasant things to plague me at Cold Creek,' she said mysteriously. 'I will be happier here.'

'In that case,' Luke said simply, 'I'm glad you're here. Thank you for showing me around.'

CHAPTER EIGHT

ONE WICKED BLOW

Number Three bridge, being so close to camp at Rancheria Flat, was in no danger of molestation. But Luke kept guards at Number One and Number Two. Keno Udell was working out of the Flat now and Luke met him one evening. 'Any luck, Keno?'

The restless little rider shrugged. 'I've hit some sign a couple of times, but it seems to fritter out on me just when I'm beginnin' to get warm. They're smart, plenty smart. But so's a coyote. And I never lost a coyote yet, once I set my mind plumb to gettin' him.'

Luke smiled. 'You're doing a good job, Keno. Since you've been riding the sage we haven't had a lick of trouble.'

'Don't stop guardin' those bridges, Luke,' warned Keno seriously. 'We ain't skinned this critter yet.'

'Not yet, Keno. But we will.'

'Ain't your time gettin' pretty short?'

'Yes, it is. But so is the trail ahead. Once we get past Number Four bridge we'll really make time. And while we do, you keep on riding and looking and listening.'

'Them,' said Keno 'are the things I do best.'

Steel moved and left Rancheria Flat behind.

The gorge and Number Four bridge lay just ahead. Here was rock and more rock and the dogged crews called often and continuously on the lethal power that came in boxes, packed in sawdust. Those slick, dirty brown sticks, wrapped in waxed paper. The stuff that could shatter and move mountains. Dynamite! And the voice of it roared and rumbled and sent the echoes rolling with increasing frequency.

Dick Leslie literally lived at Number Four. First there in the morning, last to leave at night. Number Four grew and took shape and grace and strength. While steel pushed up to meet the completion of the bridge.

John Guthrie came in from Cold Creek and established his headquarters at Rancheria Flat. To Luke he said, with obvious satisfaction, 'Everything is cleaned up at the Cold Creek end. The balance of our steel is at Garnet and coming in steadily. We have no more worries there. And the other odds and ends have all been taken care of. From here on in to the finish I can live with this end of the job and it's something I've been looking forward to all along. I can now take some of the weight off your shoulders, Luke. And I hope you don't mind my saying that you've done miracles.'

Luke shrugged. 'Not me, John. Those men out there. You'd think they were clawing their way through to heaven, the way they put out. I feel like tipping my hat every time I pass one

165

of them.'

After looking over the work on Number Four, Guthrie told Luke, 'That youngster, Dick Leslie, is definitely headed for big things. He has imagination and ingenuity, yet he is utterly sound in engineering fundamentals. And he has one of the finest heads for figures I've run across. When this job is done he will carry away with him my unqualified recommendation.'

That evening Luke dropped over to the Leslie cabin. Dale was there alone. The moment Luke entered he was struck with the fact that the girl seemed tense and on edge, with a faint cloud of worry shadowing her fine eyes. Luke asked for Dick and the girl said, 'He's at one of the bunkhouses talking over some angle of bridge construction with some of his gang. If you want to leave word—?'

'It can wait,' Luke told her. 'I just wanted to deliver a fine pat on the back to the boy.' And he went on to relate what John Guthrie had said. 'To all of which,' he ended, 'I subscribe one hundred per cent.'

He saw the tense lines in Dale's face soften momentarily. 'I'm very happy for Dick's sake,' she said simply. 'He's worked very hard and it means a great deal to him. But then, you've all worked like slaves. Sometimes I wonder if it's worth it, if it's entirely fair. The way you work, the way Dick works, the way all the men work. I watch the men coming back to camp in the evening, numbed and almost stumbling from this unending stark, brute labor. They are silent, too drunk with weariness even to talk. Yet out they go the next morning for another driving day of the same. This thing is like an obsession with all of you. And to what end? Why just to save money for other men, so that other men may profit. Luke, I wonder if it's fair?'

It was the first time she had ever used his given name and the realization of this ran through Luke in a quick, bright lift of feeling. Yet he saw she had been utterly unconscious of the fact. She was looking past him, her eyes shadowed.

'Don't worry about those men out there,' Luke told her. 'They wouldn't miss being in on this job for the world. For it's one of those things. It's a challenge, and most men love a challenge. It adds point and purpose to their efforts. A challenge given and accepted means a fight begun. The men in the gangs don't have to work like they do. But they want to. They want to whip that deadline.'

'But what have they really to gain?'

'Satisfaction. Lord knows that the lives of those men are drab enough. Nothing behind them but dogged toil and nothing ahead of them but more of the same. Yet they have their spark of pride, every one of them. To tackle a tough job against time and whip it is something they can always look back on with satisfaction even though they get nothing out of the job personally but their wages. In various bunkhouses on jobs I've been on across the country I've listened to construction men talk and swap experiences. They never talk of ordinary jobs that entailed no special challenge. But the tough jobs, the fighting jobs, these are the ones recalled and talked over again and again. A job like this one puts a hallmark on the men who took part in it. It gives them standing among their fellows. This is the kind of a job that brings proof of achievement. And such things are vital to a man's self-respect.'

'I can understand all that,' admitted Dale Leslie. 'Yet—'

'Yet—what?'

She drew a deep breath. 'Very well. I'm afraid.'

'Afraid? Of what?'

She shrugged her slim shoulders almost feverishly. 'Of nothing—and of everything. Don't relax guarding anything for a moment, Luke—not for a moment.'

Luke would have questioned her further along this line, but realized if he did so it would serve no purpose other than to upset her still more. He reasoned that if there was more she wanted to tell, she would do so without further urging or prompting on his part.

'We're keeping our eyes open, Dale,' he

reassured her. 'Don't upset yourself with useless worrying. It's only natural for all of us at this stage of the game to begin seeing hobgoblins behind every rock and sagebush. If there is any worrying to be done, leave it to those who are being paid for it.'

She looked at him steadily and her face relaxed into a smile. 'At least we are becoming better acquainted, Luke Fenimore. Which is something.'

'It means a great deal to me, Dale.'

The gentle inflection he placed on her name brought swift color to her face. 'We live and learn, don't we?' she said. 'Well, I'll see that Dick hears what you've told me. It will make him beam with pride like a little boy.'

The next morning Luke put a different guard on Number Two and brought Flick Lee up to guard Number Four, even though it lacked completion and was not yet ready for steel.

Toward midday Alec Craigie brought the Simcoe snorting into Rancheria Flat and then on up to the head of steel. Down out of the cab stepped a tall, easy-moving figure with keen eyes and a fighting jaw.

Luke looked, then hurried over. 'Mr. Garland! I've been wondering when I'd hear from you. This is mighty fine, your visit.'

Warren Garland chuckled as they shook hands. 'To tell the truth, Luke, you and your cussed little narrow-gauge brat of a railroad

169

have been on my mind a lot. What with that deadline you're working against beginning to loom up like Kipling's thundering dawn across the bay, I've been all in a stew over your chances of beating it. I knew the only way I'd fully satisfy myself was to come out and see. How about that deadline?'

'It is,' admitted Luke frankly, 'beginning to haunt me, too. It's going to be awfully close. If our luck holds, we should make it. There isn't much room for error, though. In other words, we have our worries.'

Warren Garland nodded. 'I can understand that, all right. But there's one worry you can lay for good, Luke. That Corinth steel trouble is closed up. As soon as my road's legal staff began to do a bit of investigation, somebody got the wind up, bad. At any rate the injunction was quashed and the arrest warrants for you and young Leslie chucked in the fire. Judge Whorly made a trip in clear from Viault to assure me on that score. All of which struck me as being so queer I had our legal boys dig a little deeper. Now who do you think turns out to be the main stockholder in that old White Queen Mine?'

'Lord! I couldn't even guess!' exclaimed Luke.

'None other than Mr. Henry Shard,' said Garland dryly.

'Henry Shard! Why, that hardly makes sense.'

170

'It didn't to me either—not by itself,' admitted Warren Garland calmly. 'In fact, it looked so cockeyed I sent the legal boys into checking a whole flock of angles and what they have finally turned up is enough to startle the natives. Such as this. Jack Fargo is just a front man for Henry Shard. It was Shard, using Fargo for a front, who tied up that Grasshopper steel you folks were after. And Henry Shard is the one who really owns the freighting outfit that you've been believing all along belonged to Fargo. And as if that wasn't enough, here is the big bombshell which, happily, clears up the whole picture.'

Luke passed a hand in front of his eyes. 'I hope something clears up. Right now I'm in a deep fog, fighting my head. Go on, man—go on!'

'Very well. You understand, of course, that Shard and Ames and Leffingwell have been borrowing against the subsidy to finance construction of your road. Leffingwell and Ames in good faith, but Shard apparently with his tongue in his cheek, for the picture, as I get it, is that Shard has slyly seen to it that word has gone out to the banks that it is very doubtful that the deadline would be met and the subsidy won. Which naturally has spooked the banks considerably, and made them only too glad to get out from under by selling those loans to Mr. Jack Fargo.'

Now Luke was beginning to see a glimmer

171

of what was shaping up. 'And that, of course, goes right back to Henry Shard again, doesn't it?' he growled. 'Now at last a number of things which had me puzzled are beginning to take shape—why Shard has bucked me and every suggestion I've made since coming on this job; why the freight wagons keep rolling; why Shard messed up deliveries of steel from the mills. Mr. Garland, that damned old polecat is out to own himself a railroad that other men have paid to build.'

'Exactly!' nodded Garland. 'It's obvious that the subsidy isn't enough to pay all construction costs. It was voted only as a percentage of the cost. For their share of the balance, Ames and Leffingwell have had to dig deep into their pockets. Now, just for the sake of argument, say you miss the deadline by a mile or two. No subsidy is paid. Shard owns the loans made against it. He calls them, against Leffingwell and Ames. They must meet the loans or Shard takes the road. He completes the last short stretch of construction, takes his freight wagons off and then every ounce of freight between Castle Mountain and Garnet travels over Shard's railroad. I can imagine how he'd make Ames and Leffingwell pay through the nose. Altogether, Luke, I'd call it as fine a little game of freeze-out as I ever ran across.'

'Ames and Leffingwell would have to meet those notes, wouldn't they?' mused Luke. 'And they must be personal notes if the only collateral put up was the promise of the subsidy. Why, if Curt Leffingwell and Frank Ames couldn't produce the money, Shard could force them to the wall, bankrupt them, seize their mines.'

'Something like that,' agreed Warren Garland. 'Strictly a case game, I'd call it. For if Ames and Leffingwell *were* able to meet the notes, Shard would still own his third of the road and would get back the money he advanced buying up the notes.'

'But he'd still be out his third of the expense which the subsidy wouldn't take care of,' stated Luke. 'And he wouldn't like that. From what I've seen of Henry Shard, he's a sure-thing gambler. I'll bet right now that Ames and Leffingwell wouldn't be able to meet those notes, and Shard knows it.'

'Shouldn't wonder,' nodded Garland. 'In which case, as you say, Shard not only ends up full owner of the railroad, but he can push Ames and Leffingwell to the wall and grab their mines. Offhand, I'd say the fellow was about as thoroughgoing a scoundrel as I've come across in a long, long time.'

'Curt Leffingwell and Frank Ames must know these things right away,' said Luke. 'Mr. Garland, I don't know how we're ever going to make it up to you, for all you've done to help us. If we do put this job across it will be as much due to your efforts as to any of our own.'

Garland grinned. 'I love to see a rascal

nabbed by the short hair, Luke. And I thought at this stage of the game it might be a pretty sound move to let you folks know just who your real enemy is. Give Ames and Leffingwell my best regards.'

*　　　*　　　*

Castle Mountain was a misnomer. There wasn't any castle and there wasn't any mountain. There was just a gulch and along one side of it clung the buildings of the town, clustered about a single street. Higher up the gulch were the mine buildings, with shaft derricks rising gaunt and stark. Tailing dumps fanned out, raw and unlovely. Beyond the mines were the smelters, their stacks giving out a thin, fume-choked, offensive smoke. Wealth lay here, but no beauty.

Luke Fenimore rode up the street, still-faced and alert. Dozens of mountainous freight wagons stood here and there, particularly up by the smelters. There was one little side street, more of an alleyway in fact, which held a hitching rail. Here Luke left his horse and went on afoot. A white-aproned bartender stood with arms akimbo in the doorway of a saloon, blinking at the sunlight as though his eyes were unused to such brightness. Of him Luke asked, 'Where might I find Frank Ames or Curt Leffingwell, friend?'

174

The bartender pointed. 'That's Ames' office yonder. He's there most of the time.'

Luke found himself in an outer office presided over by a thin-faced, sleek-haired clerk, a bumptious sort who gave Luke the barest flicker of attention while engrossed in manicuring his nails with offensive care.

'Frank Ames in?' Luke asked.

The clerk yawned. 'Busy.'

A rasp came into Luke's tone. 'Tell him that Luke Fenimore wants to see him—and that it's important.'

The clerk quit yawning, forgot his fingernails. 'Guess he ain't too busy. Go right on in.'

Luke went into the inner office and found Ames and Leffingwell both there. Ames exclaimed, 'Luke Fenimore! Glad to see you, Luke.' Then, at the look on Luke's face, Ames sobered quickly. 'Something has gone wrong?'

'Could be,' said Luke. 'We'll see.'

In the outer office the sleek-haired clerk went quietly out and hurried down the street.

Luke laid it on the line, all of it, just as Warren Garland had given it to him. When he finished, Frank Ames was staring straight ahead, all the usual good nature strained out of his round, rosy face. Curt Leffingwell was on his feet, pacing back and forth, shaking with anger. As Luke finished speaking, Leffingwell brought up violently.

'We deserve it, Frank. We sure do,' he

175

gritted. 'We deserve it for ever being blind enough to trust Shard, that miserable, scheming, damnable old rat. How could we have been so infernally blind, not to have suspected something like this long ago? So many things have been there to warn us, if we'd had the sense of chickadees. Great God! How could we have been such monumental fools?'

'He messed up the steel orders from the mills,' droned Frank Ames woodenly. 'He argued against going after that Corinth steel, when it was a must—when it was that or go under without a gasp. He tried to keep us from hiring Luke here. He tried to keep us from firing Runnell. There have been a hundred signs which should have warned us, Curt—and we never saw through a single one of them. All the time we thought he was merely a penny-pinching, super-cautious old fool. And he was really outthinking and outsmarting us at every jump. You're right, Curt—we've been the world's biggest idiots.'

'We deserve it, Frank,' groaned Leffingwell. 'We deserve all we get.'

'And we'll get it,' nodded Ames. 'There is just one thing that can save us. I guess you know what that is, Luke.'

'The subsidy?' asked Luke. 'Things are really that bad?'

'Yep—that bad. For when Shard calls those notes, unless we have that subsidy jackpot to draw on, Curt and I are sunk. I haven't enough reserve to meet the notes. Neither has Curt. Shard can smash us completely. He can take our mines.'

Curt Leffingwell swung a savage arm. 'That's right,' he snarled. 'For the money Shard put out to buy up those notes, he can get our mines and win full control of a railroad which he only put up a third to build. He ends up with everything—Frank and I with nothing.'

It was Frank Ames who recovered first, managed a twisted grin. 'I guess that puts it strictly up to you and your boys, Luke. You got to beat that deadline. Everything Curt and I own to our names is riding on that fact.'

'And pass out this word, Luke,' vowed Leffingwell. 'There's a bonus of a month's wages for every man on the job if the deadline is beaten.'

'A bonus isn't necessary to get the boys to do their best, Curt,' said Luke. 'Yet I'll tell them. Now I'd like to suggest something. Don't you and Frank go charging down on Shard with blood in your eye. Let him keep on thinking he is putting something over on us. He won't be as dangerous that way, as he would be if you forced his hand too soon.'

'That makes sense,' agreed Leffingwell. 'Much as I'd like to get my hands on him and twist his miserable neck. Frank and I will lay low and act as stupid as we have been up to now. But once let us beat that deadline and make sure of the subsidy money and Henry Shard will really know something has hit him. Frank and I will be two to one against him and everywhere he turns we'll have him blocked. If we don't end up by hanging his crooked hide up to dry, then I'm an everlasting liar!'

Half an hour later Luke went down the street of Castle Mountain to where he had left his horse. The bartender no longer stood in the doorway of the saloon, but a number of men were grouped there, watching Luke. Luke noticed the group but for the moment thought nothing of it. Then, at the rear of the group, just inside the place, Luke glimpsed a pair of shoulders that were familiar. Bart Runnell! Instantly, though not betraying it outwardly, Luke was wary and alert.

Which served him well, for, as he reached the mouth of the alley and started to turn into it, a lank figure bumped into him, snarling a curse with a profane demand to know why he didn't look where he was going. It was a dodge so old it had moss on it and, because of the alertness that was running through Luke, it backfired.

For this fellow had a gun and was going for it, even as he cursed. Luke hit him, not as hard as he would have liked to, because he had to hit fast and with no chance to set himself. Yet there was enough behind the punch to stagger the fellow. Before he could recover Luke drove in and sent his left hand down and forward, trapping the fellow's gun hand. Luke slid his own right hand across his body along his belt, under the flap of his coat. It came away bearing the big Colt gun that had become Luke's constant companion these days.

The man lurched at Luke, trying to crowd him, to stamp down on his feet, to wrestle his gun hand free and to muffle Luke's draw. Luke brought a knee up, hard and driving, smashing it into the fellow's midriff, knocking him back. Then, his own gun free, Luke swung it, hard, whipping his man across the head with it. The fellow crumpled.

Luke got his horse and rode out into the street. He still carried his gun, naked in his hand. He stabbed it level and the report of it bellowed along the street. The slug slammed into the wall of the saloon above the door. The group of watching men scattered wildly, diving for shelter in every direction. Luke laughed sardonically and loped his horse out of town.

*   *   *

John Guthrie said, 'I don't see how Shard fooled Frank Ames and Curt Leffingwell so badly. But then, perhaps I shouldn't say that, for he had me fooled just as completely. Like Frank and Curt I had him down as a penny-pinching, pigheaded, sarcastic old blister, but I never remotely figured him to be the slick, scheming crook that he is. It seems the only

179

one he didn't fool was you, Luke.'

'On the contrary,' said Luke. 'Oh, I admit there were a number of angles I wondered about considerably, but I never once guessed the actual setup. Now, of course, everything adds up. But it took Warren Garland and his legal staff to really let in the light.'

'And now it's strictly up to us,' said Guthrie soberly. 'We beat the deadline, or else! You know, Luke, I'd hate like the devil to feel that I had helped build a railroad that Henry Shard, by slick manipulations, got full control of. That would be the bitterest of bitter irony.'

Luke nodded. 'We'll beat the deadline, John—or tear the world apart trying. We'll work day and night if we have to. How's Number Four coming along? You've been right there on the job all day.'

'The bridge will be ready when the steel gets there,' assured Guthrie. 'Once across Number Four we'll go up the clear flats beyond like a prairie fire on the loose. If only everything will hold together, Luke. Like that old Union Foundry engine. We'd be lost without that rig. How Casey O'Keefe keeps it rolling is beyond me. He and his fireman nurse the old rig like it was a baby. We got some mighty damn fine men on this job, Luke.'

'None better,' nodded Luke. 'None better— ever!'

They had been sitting on Luke's bunk, talking. Now Guthrie left and Luke turned in to try and get some sleep. He was weary, dog-weary to the very soul of him. Not so much physically, but completely drained from nervous exhaustion. Tough-fibered as he was and coolly balanced, the pressure was beginning to get him.

This was like no other job he had ever tackled before. There had been other tough ones along the line, but they had been against measurable opposition, so many yards of earth and rock to move, so many yards and miles of grade to build and steel to lay with, occasionally even time limits to meet. But never before a job that held all these and the opposition of shrewd, ruthless, scheming trickery besides. Either one of these was tough enough in itself for a man to handle. The combination of the two was hell with the gates open.

The pressure of it all was building up a wildness in him, an explosive recklessness which was as dangerous to himself as it was to others. Like that stunt of throwing a shot over the heads of that saloon gang in Castle Mountain. Viewed in afterthought, that had been a fool play. It could, thought Luke, have gotten him into no end of trouble, could have tied him up, kept him away from the job, even got him shot. Yet the fever was in him to rip and tear, to dare anything or do anything to put a crimp in the opposition and to hell with the results.

Which was dangerous thinking, not good thinking, and Luke knew it. That sort of thing could play right into the opposition's hands. For to get him off the job and keep him off it, even for a day, now, would be a victory for them. Because the days were growing short, very short.

Staring wide-eyed at the rafters above him, Luke counted off those days and mentally measured miles. The result was anything but comforting or reassuring.

That was the hell about time and distance. They were two things a man could neither stretch nor compress. A mile of distance was a mile of distance and it took exactly a mile of steel to bridge it. And there were just so many minutes and hours in a day. Time and distance, fixed and immutable and beyond the manipulations of any mortal man.

Luke realized suddenly that the muscles of his stomach were pulled into tight, quivering knots and that tension held him all over, hard and unyielding. He was even gritting his teeth. He rolled over, swearing softly, pounding his pillow, burrowing his head into it. He sought sleep grimly. When it finally came, it hit him like a club.

It was during the utterly black, chill hours of early morning that he awakened. His mind was dull and sleep-fogged, and he lay there stupidly, trying to figure out why he had awakened. As there was no answer he closed his eyes again and tried to regain the blessed state of forgetful unconsciousness. Then, far back in his mind, a little bell started ringing, and kept ringing again and again, insistent and clamorous.

Luke shook his head, scrubbed his eyes with the back of a hand, and pushed himself up on one elbow. All along the bunkhouse he heard men stirring, as though they too had been disturbed by something, some alien, warning sound that had struck through the drug of sleep and made a mark upon relaxed senses.

Listening, Luke heard the stirring cease and the slow, measured breathing of men once more sunk deep in slumber. It must be, he thought, that he was fancying things, or had been nagged into wakefulness by the mounting weight of strain over the job. He dropped back on the pillow, but found himself more wide-awake than ever, for that little bell at the back of his mind kept on jangling.

With a mutter of impatient disgust, Luke threw aside his blankets, pulled on his boots and went quietly outside, keening the moist, chill air. Rancheria Flat lay still and peaceful and sleeping. Up gorge and down, all was quiet. Overhead the stars wheeled their ageless watch. The pungent flavor of dark sage all about hung so heavy on the air it seemed he could taste it. He shivered slightly in the chill, turned to go back to bed.

The big figure of Johnny Megarry loomed

before him. 'What is it, Luke?' asked the big fellow.

Luke shrugged. 'I don't know, Johnny. Nerves, I guess.'

'Not nerves,' said Johnny slowly, 'For I have no nerves. Yet it woke me, too. A sound. It hangs in the back of my mind that it was a shot. Yes, I think it must have been a shot.'

'A shot! Who would be shooting at this time of night—or morning?'

'Well now,' replied Johnny, 'there's Flick Lee up at Number Four, and he has a rifle and your own orders to shoot first and ask questions later, should he glimpse a prowler. I'm wondering about Flick, for there's uneasiness runnin' through me.'

They stood there, staring up toward the gorge. And at that moment it came.

First it was visual. A lifting, miniature volcano of jagged light splitting the gorge, vivid and blinding. And then the tearing violence of explosion, savagely heavy, which shook the earth and sent echoes rolling like thunderclaps.

For a moment it kept Luke and Johnny standing there, dazed and shaken, Then, black foreboding of complete disaster hit Luke and stung him into voice and movement. The shout he lifted was unnecessary. That blast had everyone in the camp awake and stirring. As Luke stormed back into the bunkhouse, men were cursing and calling, 'What is it? What's happened?'

Luke tried to keep his voice steady. 'They've used dynamite on us again. Looks like they've blown Number Four. Everybody up and out— fast!'

Men boiled from their blankets, into their clothes, cursing with a sodden bitterness. Luke got gun and coat and led the men out, calling for lanterns.

There was no wait for transportation. They streamed off up the track, carrying lanterns which threw ragged, weird flickers of light. They were silent now, bleak and vengeful. A man touched Luke's elbow.

'It can't be Number Four, boss—it just can't be. For Flick Lee was guarding it, and Flick is a good man.'

'Yes, a good man,' agreed Luke dully. 'But I don't see how it could be anything but Number Four. Something could have happened to Flick.'

They reached the end of steel and hurried on, scrambling along the trail of the gorge. Now they could smell the aftermath of explosion, the raw stench of powder, the acrid breath of scorched timbers. And they knew their worst fears were justified.

At length they looked down where Number Four should have been. The gorge lay black and empty. Except, down below, where the frugal waters of the river were gurgling and splashing over against and around a torn, twisted tangle of splintered timber and shattered foundations.

A man cursed, and there was something like a sob in the sound.

Luke lifted a shout. 'Flick! Flick Lee! Where are you, Flick?'

A faint voice, muffled and indistinct, answered from across the gorge. Luke led the way over, sliding, scrambling, leaping. He called again and the reply led him to the far side of a big boulder. The probing rays of Luke's lantern showed the figure of a man lying there. Luke lowered his lantern and dropped on one knee. He could hardly believe his eyes. It wasn't Flick Lee lying there. It was John Guthrie!

One of Guthrie's legs was doubled and twisted back in a way that told its own story. On the front of his shirt was a dark, soggy blot. Blood trickled from a corner of his mouth.

Luke snapped out of his daze, bent close over Guthrie. 'John—John! What happened? You're here—how?'

Guthrie's lips moved slowly. 'Listen close—Luke. Not—much time. I couldn't sleep. The bridge—was on my mind—for some reason. I came up here—found Flick Lee and sat—talking to him. There wasn't a sound—the night completely still—empty. They must have come in on us—like snakes. Then—guns went off—behind us. Got me center—through and through. Don't know what happened to Flick.

They—'

John Guthrie coughed weakly and went on, his voice faint and losing all substance. 'They came rushing in—then. Four of them. Carrying dynamite—plenty. Figured I was dead—I guess. Heard them talking—back and forth and identified them by their—voices. Four of them. Fargo—Ogard—Bole Ives—and—and Bart Runnell. Don't forget—those four, Luke. Don't forget. They lit—fuses—cleared out. I heard—horses running. Then—the blast. Something hit—my leg. Can't feel it—now. Can't feel anything—anything—'

Guthrie's voice died out. Luke moved his lantern closer. Guthrie's eyes were closed. 'John!' blurted Luke hoarsely. 'John!'

It was Johnny Megarry, moving in by Luke, who knelt and laid an ear over John Guthrie's heart. He straightened slowly, his big, honest face working.

'Gone?' asked Luke dully.

Johnny Megarry nodded silently.

They found Flick Lee some twenty yards away, where the force of the blast had thrown him. But Flick had been dead before the blast, and never felt it. For Flick had been shot through the back of the head.

CHAPTER NINE

A DEBT SETTLED

They waited for the dawn with stunned, almost apathetic eyes. Not a man needed to be told that here was catastrophe indeed. Here was defeat. Here, in splintered, riven timbers, in the wicked deaths of men good and true, were the very ashes of defeat. Their still, black fury was of little good to them. Time had them by the throat. Time, the remorseless one!

Through that pale dawn a man came riding, a little, restless, tireless man. Keno Udell. He sought out Luke and said quietly, 'I've found the skunk den. It was empty, but the smell is there. They'll be back. Shall we go get them, Luke?'

Here was something to do, something besides standing and staring at mocking defeat. Here could be retribution, revenge, something to relieve the racking, consuming bitterness. Luke's head came up. 'Why, yes, Keno,' he answered tonelessly. 'Yes—we'll go get them. There are horses and guns at the Flat. We'll leave right away.'

They went back to the Flat, caught and saddled horses, loaded rifles and prepared to leave. There was Luke and Keno and Johnny Megarry. There was Casey O'Keefe and his fireman, Herc Powell. There was an old-timer, Tex Ricker, who had been a bunkie of Flick Lee's. And, just as they were swinging up, came Dick Leslie.

Luke said, 'No, Dick. I've made a mess of everything else. I'm not going to have you stop a slug to top matters off. You stay here. No argument!'

Johnny Megarry said 'Once there was a deadline to beat—a subsidy to win. Once those things seemed awful important, didn't they, Luke? Now they don't seem to matter at all.'

'To hell with subsidies and deadlines!' Luke grated harshly. 'We got something a lot bigger and more important to do. Lead off, Keno!'

Keno Udell led off, a little man whose observing senses were never still, never at rest. The general direction was a little south of east. The miles fell behind them, in a wilderness of rolling earth and endless sage. Never once did Keno Udell waver in his choice of direction, never did he hesitate. He was like a homing pigeon, flying straight to its cote. He spoke just once.

'I calc'late them hombres won't head straight for their hangout. They'll ride a big circle, figgerin' to fade out their trail in the sage. We have any luck, we'll be waitin' for 'em when they drift in. Lather up them bangtails, you fellers.'

The sun came up, burning hot and still. Dark patches of sweat began to dapple the

189

hides of the horses. They rode in complete silence, the only sounds the clump of hoofs, the creak of saddle, the dragging swish of sage against their stirrups.

The strangest feeling he had ever known came over Luke. He felt almost disembodied, as though he were moving in a vacuum. Everything he did was instinctive, mechanical. His mind seemed frozen, locked. All sensation left him. He felt no weariness; he had not been conscious of the early morning chill, nor the increasing heat of the sun. He saw space and sage, but no detail. The sky was there, the earth was here. He moved under the one, over the other, but was conscious of neither. Something vital had gone out of him, leaving him empty and formless.

Midmorning found them angling up the slope of a long ridge, with sage and cedar lifting tall and thick along the crest. Just short of that crest, Keno Udell reined in and slipped to the ground. 'Wait here,' he said.

He climbed to the crest, and disappeared in that thick line of sage. In a few minutes he was back. 'Keno!' he said, with satisfaction. 'They ain't got back yet. That'll give us a chance to show 'em that two can play at this game of surprises. We'll leave the broncs here.'

On foot they followed him up and over the top and into the heavy mat of brush. They dropped down the opposite slope and when the sage thinned abruptly, Keno Udell stopped and pointed. 'That's it.'

Below, in the bottom of a narrow gulch, stood the warped, sagging, sun-bleached buildings of an old mine. There was a fairly extensive tailing dump, now overgrown with sage. The place looked utterly deserted.

'Lookin' down from that ridge yonder, you can't see a darn thing of that layout,' said Keno. 'Which is why I kept missin' it up to now. Two or three times I been on top of yonder ridge and never knowed what was down below. I had to git a look from the north side to locate it. The trail they use in and out, comes from over southeast. Now let's git down there and have ourselves settled and waitin'. They'll be along.'

One of the buildings was an old combined cook and bunk shack. Here were four bunks with blankets, a supply of food and other signs of recent habitation.

Keno Udell said, 'Our best play is to hunker down by the tailin' dump. That stuff will stop lead. This'—and he drove a boot toe against the flimsy wall of the building—'won't stop a handful of birdshot.'

They found places along the dump on the upgulch side, and watched the lower approach with grim eyes. Said Keno Udell again, 'This thing can maybe turn powerful brisk. I never like to go into a fight with my hands any way tied. Jest how far do we go with them coyotes, Luke?'

191

For a moment or two, Luke Fenimore didn't answer. He thought about Dale Leslie—and Bart Runnell. Once there had been a definite attachment there, just how serious he couldn't tell. Since Dale Leslie had come to Rancheria Flat she had been a different person. She never mentioned Bart Runnell, nor did she seem to miss him. But whether friendship or a stronger feeling lay between the girl and Runnell, Luke could not be certain. Sometimes there was no telling how a woman's mind worked.

But Luke thought further than this. He remembered how John Guthrie had looked, lying there in the Castle River gorge, shot through the back, dying, beaten and shattered by the blast. With his last words John Guthrie had named four men and asked Luke not to forget any one of those four. One of them had been Bart Runnell.

Then there was Flick Lee, poor little old Flick Lee, doughty and faithful. They had shot Flick through the back of the head. And beyond Flick Lee and John Guthrie was all of the whole crooked, scheming, backbiting layout, from Henry Shard down.

Luke cleared his voice harshly and said, with cold deliberateness, 'We didn't come out here to swap words with those whelps, Keno. We came to clean out a rattlesnake nest. So, we go all the way. All the way! Only, before they get it I want them to see us and know who is giving it to them and why. I want them to realize that John Guthrie and Flick Lee are riding with us.'

'Keno!' said the little man, and he spat through his teeth.

Time went by slowly. They didn't talk any more. They just crouched there, waiting. Keno Udell was at the outer point of the dump where, through a gap in the sage, he could watch the lower approach. He was motionless, reflecting a patience without limit. And all the time he listened and looked, never missing a thing that moved.

Luke felt dry and harsh inside. The first numbing shock was wearing off. Yet the driving activity of the past few weeks seemed dim and far away, somehow pointless and of little moment. For it had only led to John Guthrie and Flick Lee, lying dead there in the river gorge. Good men, both, who had died because they had tried to build, to create. There didn't seem to be any real balance to the world, any point to a man's striving and working, when it could all end so uselessly and at such cost. If there were any values at all, they were crazy and unreal.

Luke shook himself, trying to switch his droning thoughts to some saner level. For if this sort of thinking persisted, he would find himself hating Frank Ames and Curt Leffingwell and their whole damn railroad. He remembered the talk he had had with Dale Leslie, the things she had said. How she wondered if it were fair for men to toil and slave so mightily, so that other men might benefit, might make more money.

Even Henry Shard. He mustn't forget Henry Shard—no, never forget Henry Shard. For in the background though he was, Henry Shard was to blame for all this. He was to blame for—

'Here they come!' said Keno Udell quietly. 'Take a look, Luke.'

Luke eased over beside the little man, had his look. 'Yeah,' he muttered savagely, 'here they come—all four of them.'

They were riding two abreast. In the lead were Jack Fargo and Cob Ogard, in the rear Bole Ives and Bart Runnell. They rode relaxed and easy, talking idly together. At something Bole Ives said, Luke heard Bart Runnell laugh.

Without turning his head, Luke said to his companions, 'Get ready! I'm going to move out into the open. I want them to see me. Then they'll know why the rest follows.'

'Don't take a chance, Luke,' growled old Tex Ricker. 'Just smoke 'em down like the damned rats they are. They deserve nothing else.'

'No, they don't,' agreed Luke. 'But they must know, before they get it, that this is for John Guthrie and Flick Lee. So it'll be like I say. Watch yourselves. They're coming close.'

The four had to pass the end of the dump to reach the old bunkhouse. They were not over thirty yards distant when Luke Fenimore stepped into the clear. His voice cut at them, as toneless and thin and dry as the wind of death.

'For John Guthrie and Flick Lee. Now, damn you, you know why!'

For one spellbound, breathless second, they stared, stupefied at sight of Luke and at the sound and meaning of his words. Cob Ogard, frowsy, bewhiskered, gorilla-bodied, snarled his desperate hate, spurred his horse into a wild, spinning leap, trying to throw up a gun at the same time. And Keno Udell cut him out of the saddle with an efficiency as smooth as it was deadly.

Luke beat Jack Fargo to it by a full half second and the wallop of the slug knocked Fargo far back over the cantle of his saddle, where he hung loosely for a moment, his arms flailing the air without meaning or purpose. Then he fell clear, limp and gangling.

Bole Ives, gross and flabby, his loose jaw dropping, his eyes staring wide in terror, shook all over at the blast of the guns, then bent slowly forward in his saddle as though making a deliberate bow. Only the bow never stopped. Ives kept right on leaning forward until he poured out of the saddle and landed on his head.

Bart Runnell had time to whirl his horse and make a run for it. But within three jumps of the terrified horse, Tex Ricker had Runnell over the sights and was pressing the trigger. The tough old Texan watched Runnell's riderless horse racing down the gorge, then patted the breech of his smoking rifle.

'A damn good-shootin' gun—this,' he said harshly.

*   *   *

They came down directly out of the sage into Rancheria Flat. The Flat seemed quiet, almost empty. But there was smoke lifting from the chimneys of the cook shacks. Luke Fenimore dismounted, turned and walked away from the others, going over to the bunkhouse and along it to his own bunk, on which he dropped, his head in his hands. He felt a thousand years old and just as useless.

The bunkhouse was empty, save for himself and a couple of bluebottle flies, droning close up to the warm rafters. Luke's mind seemed frozen, his thoughts blurred and indistinct. They ran together, making no point or profit of anything. He wondered if he'd ever be able to rest again, for now, suddenly, he was more weary than he'd ever been before in his life.

It was a grinding, aching weariness, numbing and stupefying. There was no spark in him anywhere. He was burned out, dry as a husk. In years past there had been times when he'd been down, low and discouraged, moments when life had seemed pretty bleak

196

and empty. But never had he known such a moment as this. Then at least there had been a remnant of dogged stubbornness which made him know that somehow, someway he'd climb back up again, put his feet once more on the trail. But now . . .

He had no idea how long he sat there, hunched and bleak and whipped, before someone spoke his name.

'Luke!'

He looked up, dazedly. He had not heard her come in, but there she was. Dale Leslie, very grave and still of face.

He said, his voice hard and dead and deliberately brutal, 'Bart Runnell is dead. So is Fargo and Ogard and Bole Ives. We shot them down deliberately, just like they did John Guthrie and Flick Lee. Yeah, they're all dead the four of them. The same four John Guthrie named to me before he died. The four who killed him and Flick Lee and then blew Number Four on us. They're dead—all of them. But that won't bring back—John and Flick.'

His head dropped in his hands again.

She was silent so long that the thought ran through Luke's churning mind: 'She was fond of Runnell and the word that he's dead has broken everything for her. That was a dirty-dog way of breaking the news to her, Fenimore. Just the same, it was right that Runnell should die as he did. He deserved no better.'

Dale Leslie began to speak and her voice was level and steady. 'So John Guthrie and Flick Lee have been avenged. But the job they died for is still there. And their sacrifice will be an empty one, if you quit now, Luke.'

'Quit!' mumbled Luke stupidly. 'Quit—what?'

'The job, of course. The big job. There are still things to do, objectives to attain. The railroad to be completed, the deadline beaten, the subsidy won. Yes, Luke, how about the railroad—our railroad?'

'To hell with the railroad,' Luke grated.

'So!' said Dale Leslie. 'That's the way it is, eh? The fighting man whipped at last. The trouble shooter, the man John Guthrie brought in to do the job nobody else could do, is just a quitter after all. Luke Fenimore, the miracle man! And the job John Guthrie and Flick Lee gave their lives for is to be dropped, discarded, abandoned—by the miracle man who is ready to quit when the going gets toughest. Yes, just a quitter, after all. I—thought better of you than that, Luke Fenimore.'

'You're not thinking at all,' blurted Luke, stung and smarting from her words, 'You're not using your head. Six miles of steel to lay. Two days and a half to go, and no bridge across the river. Some things are possible, some are not. Only a fool refuses to recognize the impossible!'

Now she flared, furiously angry. 'Then,' she cried, 'I'm a fool and Dick is a fool and all of those slogging, faithful men in the gangs are fools. For they're out there working now, while you sit here with your head in your hands, quitting! Yes, they're out there working—not just for Frank Ames and Curt Leffingwell—but to win for you, the man who led them so valiantly so far. But who, it seems, is ready to desert them now! They're working to win for the memory of John Guthrie and Flick Lee. Joe Keller is back on the job, his arm in a sling, still weak and far from well—but back on the job just the same. And you—you would quit—quit—!'

The very fury of her words brought him to his feet, staring at her. Her head and shoulders were back, her eyes bright with tears, her spirit flaming. Luke scrubbed his face with his hands, stared at her again. 'On this job, to miss by fifty feet is just as bad as missing by ten miles,' he rasped harshly. 'It's failure, just the same.'

'Failure!' she jeered. 'Isn't there anything else you can think of but failure? Why not think of winning—winning?'

'Six miles to go,' snarled Luke. 'Six miles—and no bridge across the river. And only two days and a half left of time. Don't you understand about time? Time—that never stops moving, that never waits one thin

199

damned second. Time—that eats at your brain, that tears at your heart, that whips you and drives you and mocks you through every cursed minute of the day and night. Time—that won't let a man sleep nights and gnaws and gnaws at him all through the day. What do you know about time? Well, I do—I know—plenty!' He was panting hoarsely when he finished.

Luke didn't see the tears in her eyes. He only knew that her voice still lashed at him. 'The night hours can be used for work, too—for work. I heard the men volunteering to Dick—saying they were willing to work night and day. No sleep—no sleep for any of them, until the job is done. Those men are out to win, not fail. They believe they can win. And of all of them there is just one quitter. You, Luke Fenimore—you!'

He caught her by the arms, shook her roughly. 'That will do,' he gritted. 'Don't you call me a quitter again. Even from you I won't take that. You've told me other things. Once you held Bart Runnell's head in your arms while you told me you'd hate me forever and ever, because I'd given the dirty whelp a beating. And now—'

'Who was Bart Runnell?' she cried. 'Someone I knew a long, long time ago and who wasn't worthy and can now be forgotten. But you—you're either a quitter, or you're not. The next sixty hours hold the answer. Luke

Fenimore, fighting man—or quitter. We shall see!'

She was right there in front of him, in the grasp of his hands, his fingers gripping so hard as to leave bruises. This girl he had so long worshiped. She was flaming, she was scornful, she was glorious. Her words had dug deep, deeper than she knew, hurting him more than a physical blow. And they had awakened something almost akin to ferocity in him. He jerked her close to him and kissed her, savagely. Then he thrust her aside so violently she almost fell. He went out of the bunkhouse at a lurching run.

Out there, snorting and clanking, the old Union Foundry engine had come down from the north and pulled to a stop. Dick Leslie was at the throttle. Behind the engine was a single flatcar, loaded with boxes of dynamite and bundles of long drills.

Casey O'Keefe and Herc Powell climbed into the cab of the engine. Others were scrambling on to the flatcar. As Luke Fenimore swung up, Dick Leslie started to speak, saw the look on Luke's face and said nothing. Luke snarled, 'Get this damn thing rolling!'

He stood erect, balancing against the lurch and sway. 'Quitter!' he muttered, 'Quitter—she called me. We'll see—we'll see!'

From the door of the bunkhouse, Dale Leslie watched the engine and car wind from

201

sight up the gorge. There were bruises on her arms that ached. The soft crimson of her lips stung and burned. But through the tears that ran down her cheeks she was smiling.

*　　　*　　　*

A great shoulder of rock blocked the eastern side of the gorge. Number Four bridge had been built to enable the road to skirt this rock shoulder. But Number Four was now a smashed-up tangle of timbers, water-slimed and dripping, leaving a gaping void which, to Luke Fenimore's embittered, burning eyes, looked as wide and deep and impassable as the depths of his own weary discouragement.

Was a man a quitter if, when faced with such a thing as this, he admitted defeat? Especially when time had him by the throat, and distance, the thing you couldn't compress by one short inch, still stretched out ahead. It was all very well for Dale Leslie to call on him to fight on—but what did she know about an obstacle like this?

Luke scrubbed his hands across his eyes, shook his head to clear the weary fog. Across the face of the frowning rock shoulder and over the top of it, men were swarming. Half of them were holding and turning drills. The other half were swinging heavy sledges and the clank of steel on steel was a steady blur of metallic sound.

Men were stripped to the waist and corded muscles coiled and slid under sweat-slimed skin. They were attacking that rock shoulder with something akin to fury. They seized upon the long drills that Dick Leslie had brought up from Cold Creek, thrust them into holes already sunk as deep as the shorter drills would reach, and went on from there, sledges crashing, drills turning.

Dick Leslie had Luke Fenimore by the arm now, and was pulling him here and there, pointing and explaining. 'We sink a row of holes across the face at grade level. We sink another row across the top, far enough back to give us side clearance. We put in all the powder the holes will take and we lift out the whole chunk at one shot. Then we go through.'

'Yeah,' growled Luke, 'through to what? We're still on the wrong side of the river—still without a bridge.'

'We'll cross up there beyond, at that riffle, where the bridge gang is working. We'll lay parallel timbers, heavy ones, to carry the steel. We'll have only gravel under the timbers but I have tried it and it is hard-packed. I doubt if it would hold up standard-gauge stuff. Too much weight. But I think it would hold our lighter, narrow-gauge rigs. The water will bank up against the timbers, may even come over the rails, but there is no drive to it as it is now. We've got to take the gamble that there'll be no storm come along to raise the water. It will be a sketchy, temporary rig, of course. But it should hold together long enough for us to get to Castle Mountain on time. Once that's done, we can rebuild Number Four at our leisure.'

They went up to the crossing, where the bridge gang were measuring their timbers, timbers carried up there by massed man power from the end of steel. Luke waded the riffle, testing the gravel under foot. This was no temporary sand and gravel bar, piled up by one freshet and ready to be carried off by the next one. This was a conglomerate, hard-packed and settled by the years. Many a flood water had rolled over this stuff, without affecting it greatly, one way or another. Water- and erosion-rounded rocks, set into this stuff, could not be lifted out by hand—it required the prying point of a pick or prybar to do this.

Luke stared at the crossing with grim eyes. 'A crazy layout,' he muttered. 'But just crazy enough to work. You've been using your head, kid.'

Luke went back to the drilling crew and felt a touch on his arm. It was Keno Udell. The little man said gravely, 'I hate pick-and-shovel work worse than pizen, but I can do it. I'd be afraid to swing one of them sledges for fear I'd cripple the man turning drill. But I ain't afraid to turn a drill, and I can do that. But mainly, there's a fight going on here. And me, I allus did like a fight. Luke, I want in on this. Tell me what to do.'

'There'll be a pair of us, Keno,' nodded Luke, beginning to strip off his shirt. 'Grab a drill.' He stepped up to one of the drilling crews. 'You boys take a breather. Udell and I'll spell you for a bit. All set, Keno? I've swung a sledge plenty in my time. I can still swing one.'

It was good to swing that sledge. The handle was smooth and slick from use-honest hickory. To gauge the swing, to put his weight into each blow just at the right split second, to feel the true, solid impact come up to him—this was good! And, strangely enough, just what he needed as an outlet for all that banked-up feeling within him. To feel his muscles loosen up under the oil of sweat, to flavor the hot, sage-scented air clear to the bottom of his lungs—these things drove the fog from his mind, took the bitter tautness out of him, made him human again.

Luke realized now that it had not been physical weariness that he had known, so much as it was the pressure of thought and worry and jangled nerves, honed fine and brittle by the piled-up menace of inexorable time and distance. And this slaving physical labor was release from those things and, in a strange way, comforting. Thoughts, tragically bitter ones, still rode with him, but these too, he found, grew a little blurred and indistinct and less harassing as the fine focus of concentration needed to sledge the end of that drill and to keep on sledging it pushed other thoughts aside.

And so they toiled, men against rock, against time and distance so short and so long, while the remorseless hours slipped away. Later, half blind with salt sweat, his lungs labored, Luke stepped back for a breather and Keno Udell joined him, while two rested men stepped up to take their places. And it was now that Luke was abruptly aware of a slim, black-haired figure in khaki blouse and skirt moving about among the men. She carried a bucket in each hand. To the rim of one of them hung several cups. From the other she drew broad, thick sandwiches.

Men turned drill with one hand, ate and drank with the other. They switched places with their partners, so their partners could eat and drink. From one team of drillers to another Dale Leslie moved bringing hot coffee and food. There was no stop, no letup. Men thanked her with their eyes.

She came up to Luke and Keno and under the level impact of her glance, Luke flushed. 'I'm sorry,' he blurted, 'for how I acted, down there. I must have been—half crazy.'

She said, her voice entirely matter-of-fact, 'That's all right now.'

The sun was nearly down when the last hole had been sunk. Powder men swarmed over the stubborn rock shoulder. Box after box of powder was emptied as the paper-wrapped sticks of explosive went into the drill holes and

206

were tamped. Fuses were cut, caps set and crimped. Tools were removed to safety. Men scattered to places of shelter.

Luke, pulling on his shirt as he dropped back down gorge, found Dale Leslie there. She was as she had been yesterday and the days before. As she had been before the cruel and wicked blow struck. Silently and without words, she and Luke watched the four men who were to light the fuses go about their work. As these men moved along little spurts and coils of white smoke began to dribble up behind them. They moved without apparent hurry, yet without a false motion. An air of tension began to build up through the gorge.

Now Dale Leslie's hand fell on Luke Fenimore's arm. 'Why don't they hurry—why don't they hurry?' she cried softly.

'Don't worry,' Luke told her. 'They know what they are doing. See, they're done!'

The four men came scrambling down and away from the rock shoulder, talking back and forth as they trotted down gorge in a little group, then dropping behind a protecting ledge. A breathless stillness of waiting settled over everything.

Dale Leslie stared at the distant rock shoulder, almost afraid to wink an eye, for fear she might miss something, It seemed she waited hours, holding her breath. Abruptly a thin haze of dust began to lift and spray from every inch of the rock—the rock itself seemed to bulge and expand.

Then the rocketing, ripping crash of the first shot bellowed. Other shots followed immediately in such swift succession that it seemed all the world was shaking and shuddering before the might of it.

A great bloom of dust rolled and billowed. And out of that dust boulders and chunks of riven, shattered rock arched high to crunch heavily, rattling like cannon balls off the opposite wall of the gorge, as the echoes rolled away, finally to die far out in the breathless sage.

Men swarmed into that dust like angry ants; and Johnny Megarry lifted a great shout. 'It's open boys—open! We got a gateway. Now get at it, you bullies. Here's where you show the stuff that's in you. Here's where we start the final sprint!'

CHAPTER TEN

MEN AGAINST MILES

It became nightmare without letup. An existence of stark brute labor which gripped and held every man, thrusting a challenge at him which he met with set thews and indomitable purpose. They were men in the grip of a splendid frenzy.

208

Steel moved up and past the ripped-out rock shoulder through the blue shadows of early dark, with a hundred lanterns to light the way. The grade gang, slashing open the softer side of the slope of the gorge, set a path for steel to the fair, open flatlands beyond with only the wide, shallow riffles of the river to bar the way.

Here the bridge gang had already laid the heavy timbers athwart the waters, anchoring them with steel drills driven deep into the hard-packed conglomerate, while steel rails ran along the length of the timbers, spiked and gauged and true. It was a temporary, desperate make-shift, but if it worked then there might still be a chance, still a faint thread of hope.

To light their work in the darkness the gangs not only used lanterns but augmented them with roaring bonfires of sagebrush, piled high at intervals. So men fought earth and rock, fought steel, fought uncertain and tricky light. But when the gray dawn of another day seeped across the world, the last day but one in which to win or lose, Casey O'Keefe was able to ease the Union Foundry engine and two flats of steel and cross ties through the gap and up to the river riffle.

'This is it, Casey,' Luke told him. 'We'll know where we stand, right now. If you can put that rig across the river, and keep doing it, we'll have a fighting chance.'

Casey looked things over. Already the steel

209

gang were working beyond the river, having lugged ties and steel across by human strength and tenacity. The ties were laid flat on untouched earth, the rails spiked down, fishplates bolted secure. Close to a hundred yards of steel were already laid and beckoning, beyond the river. The grade and steel gangs were going ahead, ever ahead. Apparently they had supreme confidence in Casey's ability to follow them.

The thin, bitter waters of the river itself backed up above the crossing timbers, gurgled and splashed over timber and rail. Casey O'Keefe took a big chew of tobacco and reached for his throttle.

'I'll take the old girl across the hinges of hell if you say so, Luke. Wish me luck and hold on to your hats!'

Casey eased the old engine out onto the water-covered rail and timber. First the ponies, then the drivers, and then the trucks of the tender dipped in water and cut through. Luke Fenimore held his breath, without knowing it. But the conglomerate held up and the timbers held up and the old engine, with a hiss and snort which seemed almost disdainful, rolled out onto the dry steel beyond, drawing the loaded flats behind.

A growled cheer went up from the watching men. Casey O'Keefe leaned out and patted the side of the cab. 'Let no man ever laugh at her again,' he yelled. 'She's an old darlin'. Now get at unloadin' this steel and the ties, ye lazy good-for-naughts, so the O'Keefe can go back after more of the same.'

Luke Fenimore let out that held breath, stretched aching arms and shoulders and glared to the south with sunken red-rimmed eyes. 'It can't be done,' he gritted. 'But she believes it can be done. So, by glory, we'll have at it!'

It seemed impossible that the pace could pick up, that these toiling, spirit-driven men somehow, somewhere could find an additional fund of strength and reserve to carry them ahead faster than ever. Yet this was so.

Men no longer walked. They ran. The grade gang built no real roadbed. They merely stormed ahead, grubbing scattered sagebrush clumps out of the way, then went back and laid ties for the oncoming steel. For now the ground was level and hard as a plain. And somewhere out there ahead was Castle Mountain.

This quickening, driving, feverish force drew into focus about one man. Luke Fenimore. His face was gaunt and craggy. His eyes sunk far back in his head, and burned there like coals. But he had regained, in part at least, the old flair that had led these men so splendidly up to the point of the great tragedy. He was here, there, everywhere, advising, exhorting, helping. It seemed that a sort of invisible aura lay about him, touching men

211

who had gone stupid with soul-dragging weariness, lifting them up again, carrying them on and on.

They cursed the swinging sun, not because of its heat but because it wouldn't stand still, because it wouldn't give them an extra hour or two of precious light. Yet, even as the sun dropped deeper into the west, steps were taken to substitute for its light. Every available lantern was gathered, filled, its wick trimmed, its chimney polished clean and bright.

Dale Leslie took care of this chore. Most of the day she had moved up and down through the gangs, carrying her buckets of coffee and food. For the cooks had moved up from Rancheria Flat now, had built their cooking fires along the right of way. So, even if there would be no sleep, there would still be food. And for most of the day it had been Dale Leslie who carried that food and drink to the toiling men.

Now she prepared light for their unending labors. Silently Keno Udell came and helped her. She too was weary, her face drawn and sharpened with fatigue. Dick, her brother, came over to her and mumbled huskily, 'I'm afraid it isn't going to do a bit of good, Sis— not a bit of good.'

'What do you mean, Dick—not a bit of good?'

'It's like this. I've figured half a dozen times, figured every angle. And every time we come

212

out short. Not by much. Maybe not more than half a mile—or even less. But—always short. There is a limit to what men can do. Time is time, and distance is distance. That's all there is to it. And we can't compress either of them enough to win.'

She faced him almost fiercely. 'There will be no more of that kind of talk, Dick Leslie,' she cried. 'There must be no mention or thought of failure. We did not come this far to lose!'

Dick lifted one of her hands, a slim, gentle hand, now smudged with soot and grime, the soft palm red and blistered from contact with the bail of a bucket, and the handles of kerosene tins. He patted it, managed a twisted grin. 'Very well, Sis,' he said simply. 'That's how it will be.'

He went back to the job, drawn and grim, thinned down from driving work and sleeplessness.

Dale turned to Keno Udell. 'Tomorrow morning, Keno, I'll be wanting a saddled horse. Will you get one for me?'

'Lady,' said old Keno with a quaint courtesy, 'if you want the moon I'll get it for you.'

So they met the night and went through it, their second night without sleep. No man stopped, no man rested. They just went on and on. Bonfires flared and made crimson light and laid sluggish smoke, pungent and acrid across the night, and by those fires and their smoke, and by the restless flitting lanterns, could progress be measured.

And there was progress, as the stubborn miles were seized and throttled and overcome and thrust behind. From time to time, pushing up more cars of ties and steel, fishplates and spikes, the headlight of the old Union Foundry engine glaring across the sage plain like a giant Cyclopean eye, Casey O'Keefe would lean from his cab window and send his wild Irish yell echoing.

'Root, you terriers—root!'

Men who were half staggering, men who were weaving in their tracks, would steady and straighten and roar their challenge back at him. 'Bring up the steel—bring up the steel!'

Then Casey would seize his whistle cord and let the old engine bay through the night.

Midnight and then the cold black sodden hours of early morning. Then dawn, pale and gray and wondering. Dawn of the final day—the day that had been almost comfortably distant a few short weeks before, but now was here, growing about them. Time had brought this day to them, tossed it in their laps. Time, the remorseless one. And where was Castle Mountain? Why, out there ahead—still out there ahead—somewhere.

*   *   *

In the clear morning sunlight of this day, this final day, Dale Leslie rode her horse into

Castle Mountain—this slim girl in khaki, with her dark, bared head shining in the sun. She viewed the sprawled, barren, thoroughly unlovely mining town with a feeling almost of resentfulness. For this was the goal of all the toil and drive and sacrifice that had been the price of the stubborn miles to the north and it would have seemed more fitting had the goal looked more worth while.

Dale found a hitching rail, dismounted, tied her horse, and then went along the street, searching for some window sign that would lead her to the man she wanted to see.

Abruptly a door just ahead of her was flung open with a crash and there was the very man she was searching for, a short, stout, rosy-cheeked little man, just now a furiously angry one. He had another man by the collar, a thin-faced, sleek-haired individual who very definitely was the worse for wear, a man rumpled and disheveled, bleeding at the mouth and with one eye rapidly swelling shut. Frank Ames gave his former office clerk a combined push and mighty kick, which sent the fellow sprawling into the street.

'There, damn you!' raged Ames. 'That's how I fire a dirty, slick, double-dealing whelp like you, Tyson. Drawing wages from me, trusted by me, yet all the time selling me out to that cursed old rat, Henry Shard. Spying on me, stealing my confidence, then peddling it to Shard. Why, blast your shriveled, stinking soul,

215

if you're not out of sight in thirty seconds I'll—
I'll—!'

Frank Ames sputtered to a stop, drew another breath, delivered another kick and went on. 'Go run to Shard! Go ahead! Tell that damned old crocodile that Frank Ames and Curt Leffingwell are wise to him, wise to all his putrid, two-faced scheming. Git! Get out of my sight before I kill you, you—!' And Frank Ames delivered himself of a sulphurous blast of scathing profanity.

The object of all this wrath and explosive advice took it literally. He stumbled to his feet and went off along the street at a staggering run. Frank Ames glared after him, stamped back, turned and saw Dale Leslie.

'Lady,' he burst out, 'I apologize for my language. I didn't realize there was a lady within hearing distance. But if you knew the breed of rat I just threw out of my office, you'd not hold it against me. Again, I apologize!'

Dale smiled. 'It's quite all right, Mr. Ames. Now, I wonder if you have time to listen to me?'

Frank Ames made a courtly bow. 'It will be my pleasure. Won't you come in?'

The outer office looked as if a hurricane had hit it. Here apparently was where Frank Ames had had his innings with his renegade clerk. But the inner office was tidy, and Dale sank into a proffered chair with an unconscious sigh of deep weariness.

'I am Dale Leslie,' she said. 'My brother, Dick, is the surveyor and construction engineer of your railroad.'

'Of course,' said Frank Ames eagerly. 'I've met him. And doing a splendid job, too, from all that John Guthrie has told me. The road— is there a chance of getting in under the wire?'

'I think so,' nodded Dale gravely. 'But only if what I have come to propose is done.'

Ames began pacing up and down his office. 'I've been waiting for Guthrie or someone to report. Curt Leffingwell and I, we've been half crazy, sitting up here, waiting, waiting. Yet, we didn't want to go down to construction, not wanting to bother or delay or take a single moment of time from any man on the job. It was Guthrie's suggestion that Curt and I do this, saying he'd keep us informed. We've been expecting some kind of word from him for the past day or two. You, perhaps, are bringing us that word?'

'I have a great shock for you, Mr. Ames,' said Dale gravely. 'John Guthrie is dead.'

Frank Ames was a man thunderstruck. He spun around, facing her, his round face pulled and bleak. 'John Guthrie—dead! You mean— John Guthrie? Great God! How—when—?'

'He was killed the night Number Four bridge was dynamited. He and Flick Lee, who was posted to guard the bridge. And the men who set the blast shot Mr. Guthrie and Flick Lee—crept up on them in the dark and shot

217

them in the back.'

Frank Ames dropped into a chair. Suddenly he was an old, tired man, his face shrunken and gray. 'John Guthrie dead—murdered, you say?' he mumbled dully. 'Shard's crowd—they did that, to ruin our chances? They murdered—killed—'

'It was Shard's crowd, all right,' Dale told him. 'Four of them. Ogard, Ives, Fargo and—and Bartley Runnell.'

Ames roused from his first stupor, his eyes burning savagely. 'They'll pay!' he burst out. 'This means that I and Leffingwell lose everything—but that doesn't matter, not now—with John Guthrie and that other poor devil—murdered. Those four—we'll go after them—we'll get the authorities—we'll see them hung to the highest tree in the state of Nevada. Before we're done with them—'

'There's no need of that, Mr. Ames,' said Dale. 'The murderers have already been punished. They were trailed and found by Luke Fenimore and Keno Udell and some of the other men. They were executed on the spot—all four of them. So, if vengeance is worth anything, John Guthrie and Flick Lee are avenged.'

'Why—why was this word not brought before?'

'I don't believe anyone took time out to think of that. You see, there was still the job to do, the deadline to beat. We—the men, once they knew the killers had paid the supreme penalty, had no time to think of anything else but the job. Time was short—so very short.'

Frank Ames lifted dreary eyes. 'I understand. But why should they care—why should they try any more? With Number Four bridge blasted—as you say it was—there isn't a ghost of a chance of winning this thing. Not a chance. For miracles just don't happen—that way. And I don't know as I care—any more. Not with John Guthrie—gone.'

He shook his head, then dropped it in his hands.

'No chance, did you say?' spurred Dale, straightening in her chair. 'Why, Mr. Ames, if you were to walk just beyond that point below this town, you could see them, see them bringing on the steel. They crossed the river above Number Four by temporary means—but they're across it, and now the crossing is far behind them.'

Ames' mind seemed numbed. 'They've done marvels—right from the first they've done marvels,' he murmured. 'I'm not questioning anything John Guthrie and Luke Fenimore and those other men have done. They've given Leffingwell and me more than we deserve. We're the ones at fault in this thing, because of our cursed blind stupidity in not seeing Henry Shard for what he was, right from the first. No, the men have done miracles, but today—well, this is the day, you know, Miss Leslie. At midnight tonight—the deadline. No—we're whipped.'

'Those slaving, fighting men out there don't think so—don't believe so, Mr. Ames,' cried Dale. 'They're coming on to win—do you understand—to win! And they can and will win if you'd just give them some help. If you just would—'

Ames' head came up again. 'I'd do anything, Miss Leslie, anything. You must know that. If only there was something I could do. But everything now is tied up in two things—time and distance. And I can't set back the hours and I can't compress the miles.'

'You can. You can cut away some of the distance. That could mean the difference between winning or losing.'

Ames shook his head wearily. 'I'm afraid I don't follow you. How?'

'By extending the town limits. That's what the deadline calls for, doesn't it? That steel and rolling stock shall be within the town limits of Castle Mountain by twelve midnight, tonight?'

Frank Ames got slowly out of his chair, began to pace the room again, a gleam of fresh new light burning the blank cloud from his eyes. 'Good Lord!' he muttered, as though to himself. 'I wonder! But why not? We'd be able to extend those limits only so far, of course. And we'd have to get Senator Ring's consent, so there'd be no kickback from the state over paying the subsidy. Then there are the city dads—and Shard!' Ames' lips twisted as he fairly spat the name. 'Shard will try and block the idea, and he has influence, with some. But would he dare show his hand so openly? If he did, he'd be advertising his crookedness to the skies, and the people of this town, who want the road badly, would go after him tooth and nail. Why, they'd run him out of town, they'd chase him out of the state!'

The gleam brightened in Ames' eyes as different angles of the picture became clearer and more vivid. 'We'll have Shard on the spot,' Ames exulted. 'We can watch him squirm and writhe and suffer—and he won't dare to fight back openly. We can jam this thing down his crooked, scheming throat.'

Ames whirled to face Dale. 'How much distance would we have to add to the limits— to have a fighting chance?'

'All we can get, of course,' Dale told him. 'But anything will help. A quarter of a mile. It will be that close, Mr. Ames,'

Frank Ames had snapped back. He said kindly, 'You are very tired, Miss Leslie. I can see that. So you stay right here and rest. I'll bring them together and then I think it would be very well for you to speak to them. Will you do that?'

'I'll be glad to,' said Dale.

221

CHAPTER ELEVEN

A WOMAN'S WITS

It was an hour later that Frank Ames led Dale Leslie into a room where some dozen and a half men were gathered. Curt Leffingwell was there and with him a tall, spare, sun-browned man with a fine head of snowy-white hair. A man with a firm jaw and keen but kindly eyes. Henry Shard was there, too, more pinched and buzzard-like of face than ever.

Frank Ames got right down to business. He outlined the pertinent facts bluntly and curtly. 'And so, gentlemen, there it is,' he ended. 'You all know what this railroad can mean to this town of ours. Three—no, two of us have taken all the financial risk, and frankly, we need that subsidy. We need it badly, Curt Leffingwell and I do. Because of a number of things that have happened, it has been growing upon Leffingwell and me, day by day, that we were going to lose the subsidy. The fault was ours, entirely, because in certain things Curt and I had been very blind. But now Miss Leslie here has brought word to us that, far from being a lost cause, the subsidy can be won, providing we of this town give those gallantly toiling men down there on the flats just a little lift. I am going to ask you to listen to Miss Leslie a

222

moment.'

Henry Shard turned his head and his cold, compressed eyes stabbed at a beefy, whisky-flushed individual. The fellow stirred and cleared his throat raspingly. 'I dunno as I can see your angle, Ames,' he said. 'But me, I ain't in favor of no fancy shenanigans that might—'

Curt Leffingwell cut in savagely, 'Speaking for yourself, Ruffert, or for Shard?'

Before the fellow could answer, it was the tall, white-haired man, State Senator Ring, who spoke up, his words crisp and biting. 'I believe Frank Ames asked that we listen to this young lady, gentlemen. For myself, I am all in favor of that, rather than listen to the mouthings of a booze-soaked, barroom bum.' Senator Ring bowed slightly toward Dale. 'If you please, Miss Leslie.'

Dale stood up. 'Thank you, Senator Ring.' She looked around the room and men watching her saw her bite her lip, saw the tears well into her eyes. But her voice came, low and clear.

'Everyone actively connected with the building of this railroad, myself included, has time and time again measured miles against hours. I have done so myself though, being a mere woman with no direct understanding of such things, I could only guess. But my brother Dick, as surveyor and construction engineer, has been in a position where, probably better than anyone else, he could figure these things

223

almost exactly. I know that he has figured them, over and over again. Just last night he came to me and told me that it was going to be close, heartbreakingly close. But short—just a little short of winning. That distance, that short measure of distance, which can mean the difference between victory or defeat—you men can help us with that. A quarter of a mile, probably less than that—that is all we are asking for.'

She paused, touched a handkerchief to her eyes, went on. 'I wish you could see, all of you, what those men down there in the gangs have done and are doing. I've seen it. I've been right with them. The way they have worked—the way they are working. The obstacles they have smashed their way through, or have overcome by sheer nerve and spirit. For two nights now, gentlemen, they have not slept. Do you understand what I mean? They are working night and day, without rest, without letup. They have not stopped for a decent meal. Look at these hands of mine!'

She held them up, showing the reddened and blistered palms. 'That comes from carrying buckets of food and drink to the men. They ate with one hand while working with the other. I don't know why they should do this—I don't know why I should. For yours is the gain, their return is so small. But it's the glorious pride in them, the bitter determination to whip the seemingly impossible, to prove that they are mightier than distance or time. They are dead on their feet. They stagger when they walk and run. Their eyes are sunken and glazed and blank from brute fatigue. But they do not stop—they keep coming. They are coming on now, gentlemen—storming up those flats below town. And they deserve victory. For they are—heroic!'

Dale choked up. She could not go on. She was seeing and understanding things these men would never really see and understand. The tears in her eyes welled over, ran down her cheeeks. A sob shook her shoulders. She sat down, deathly weary.

A stir ran through the room. Men shifted in their chairs. Senator Ring, tall, white of hair, his wind- and sun-tanned face working slightly, stepped over beside Dale and dropped a kindly hand on her shoulder. His voice rang.

'On behalf of the Governor and the state, I see no reason why you men should not extend the limits of your town a full quarter of a mile—north. And if steel crosses that line by midnight tonight, the subsidy will be paid. Now, from a purely personal point of view I want to say that if you don't get damn well busy and extend those limits immediately, you're a pack of senseless, spineless fools. Vote, damn you—and get it done with!'

A man at the rear of the room said, 'I'll vote, Senator. And I vote—yes—for the extension of the limits.'

225

'And I.'

'And I.'

'Me, too.'

It ran swiftly over the group. Only Henry Shard and two others were silent. They were whipped, and knew it.

Senator Ring bent over Dale, his eyes very kind. 'And now, Miss Leslie,' he said, 'I'd like to shake one of those little, blistered hands.'

Curt Leffingwell stalked over and faced Henry Shard. His voice was a growl. 'I have just heard that John Guthrie and one of the men named Flick Lee were killed, Shard—murdered is the proper word. Yes, murdered by men who Frank Ames and I intend and expect to prove were in your pay and employ and acting under your orders. The killers were four. Jack Fargo, Bole Ives, Cob Ogard and—Bart Runnell. I'm happy to say that these same four were run down, cornered, and shot to death in just reprisal. Now, for you—'

Leffingwell stopped abruptly, startled by the strained whiteness that whipped across Henry Shard's face. 'Not Bart—not Bart Runnell!' cringed Shard. 'Don't tell me that Bart is dead—my nephew Bart!'

'He's dead,' reaffirmed Leffingwell harshly. 'And you can play with the realization that because you sent him out with the rest of your hired thugs to do your dirty work, the responsibility for his death is yours. Also, you are equally guilty for the murder of John

226

Guthrie and Flick Lee, even though you may not have actually pulled the triggers of the guns that killed them. Frank Ames and I will prove that. As sure as there's a God in heaven Ames and I intend to put you over the road, Shard, if it is the last thing we ever do. We are going to swear out a warrant for your arrest, charging you with murder, conspiracy and the intent to defraud. Those charges will do to start with. There'll probably be others as we go along. Now let's see you wiggle off this hook, you slimy snake!'

*   *   *

They came around the point of the ridge below town in the last hours of sunshine. They looked along the remaining distance, cursed it and went after it. The minutes ticked off, the hours flew. Men gauged the position of the sun by the feel of it, not wasting time to look at it.

They had gotten through the final day. Just how, they didn't know, but they had. They were like dead men who would not fall down. Their faces were slack, their eyes glazed. They moved as though they didn't fully see. Yet, somehow, they did see.

There were bloodstains on rails and ties, blood on more than one fishplate bolted into place. But what mattered a torn, gashed or crushed finger in the midst of the final battle? There could be no pause or halt for such

227

trifles. And there were none.

Luke Fenimore had held back every thought of defeat, from the time he had stretched his arms and squared away for the final drive. He had held back such thoughts doggedly. For hadn't Dale—Dale Leslie—said it could be done? Hadn't she said so, and wouldn't she know, somehow?

Yet, panic was beginning to gnaw at him now. He fought it off. He owed it to Dale to the men—those haggard, work-drunk, indomitable devils who wouldn't be licked. They'd keep on driving, right up to the final stroke of midnight. And he'd be in there with them. A man could not win every time maybe. But if he had to lose then he would go down fighting. A man just kept on trying.

It didn't matter that his mind and sensibilities had long since gone cold and numbed and confused. It was purely automatic now. A man, it seemed, could become a machine and move and act purely by instinct. Even when the fight had clubbed all else out of him, reflex could carry him on. That, reasoned Luke numbly, must be the way of it, for there seemed to be nothing conscious at all about anything he did, now.

And so they went on, with Luke leading them, out of the last daylight, through the early dark and down the rushing hours toward midnight. By lantern and firelight, as before, they went on, while Casey O'Keefe would nose

228

the old Union Foundry engine up on to steel that had hardly stopped ringing from the last blow of the spiking sledges, and the lancing beam of the headlight furnished radiance in which men could lay and gauge and spike down more steel.

And Casey's yell would lift, hoarse and ragged now. 'Root you terriers—root!'

And they would answer him, startled by the hollowness of their own shouts. 'Bring on the steel—bring on the steel!'

So Casey would bring on the steel and the old engine whistle would scream across the flats, as though defying time and distance, as though taunting all the little, fearful men of all the world, men who would shrink at stupendous tasks, men who would not dare—!

Out there were the lights of Castle Mountain. They seemed so close they could almost reach out and touch them. But always there was more steel to go down, more distance to span.

'Root, you terriers, root!'

'Bring on the steel—the steel—!'

And the old engine, baying like a mad banshee across the night.

They didn't see the group that came down from Castle Mountain through the darkness of approaching midnight, people who streamed and crowded off to one side in that darkness, where they waited, silent and watchful—awed and breathless.

Nor did Luke and his men see the white stake that had been driven into the earth out ahead of them, even after the light of Casey O'Keefe's old engine had picked it up and brought it closer and closer.

Back in that waiting, silent group of watchers a match flickered briefly as Frank Ames looked at his watch. To Senator Ring he said, 'Just minutes away now, Senator. What do you think of them?'

Senator Ring said softly, 'This beats anything I ever saw before. I wish the Governor was here to see this finish. He'd be a proud man, proud of his state, proud of the men in it. For by God, gentlemen, that is a bunch of real men out there. You hear me? A bunch of real men. That grand girl was right. They're heroic!'

'Root—you terriers—!'

'Bring on the steel—!'

That steel crept up to the white stake, went by it. The battering clank and rattle of spiking sledges echoed steadily. Casey O'Keefe did not guess that he was making history as he nursed the throttle of his ancient engine and pushed out on to that final length of steel.

Frank Ames turned and said, 'Well Senator?'

Senator Ring said, 'That does it. The subsidy will be paid! Congratulations, gentlemen!'

'No congratulations to us, Senator—not to

230

us,' murmured Ames, looking at his watch again. 'But to those men over there. It is now seven minutes to midnight. By that much, plus the wit and courage of a grand girl, Luke Fenimore and his men have won their fight! If I was ten years younger, I'd bawl like a kid.'

*   *   *

Luke Fenimore thought that the world and all the people in it had gone suddenly stark raving crazy. For people came charging out of the darkness, caught at him, shook his hand, slapped him across the shoulder, while all the time babbling some incredible mocking nonsense about the bitter race being won, the deadline beaten, the subsidy realized.

There was Frank Ames and Curt Leffingwell, among others, with Ames introducing him to a tall man in a white sombrero, a man named Senator Ring. There was yelling and cheering and abruptly, up beyond Castle Mountain town, mine whistles began screeching and moaning. Casey O'Keefe had apparently gone as starkly crazy as everybody else and he must have tied down the whistle cord of the old Union Foundry engine, for the engine whistle was splitting the night in one long, triumphant shriek.

Luke got mad. He tried to push them aside. 'We're wasting time,' he snarled. 'You crazy, damn fools! We're wasting time. Quit holding

231

up the job. We got steel to lay!'

Then it was Joe Keller who had an arm about his shoulders. Good old Joe, with his other arm still in a sling, and Joe was saying, 'We've done. it, boy—we've won! Can't you understand? We beat the deadline!'

Luke blinked stupidly. 'Castle Mountain— it's still out there, Joe. Those lights— We haven't reached those lights!'

'No! You're wrong, Luke. Castle Mountain isn't out there. It's right here. You're standing inside the town limits of Castle Mountain right this minute, I tell you, Luke—the fight is won!'

Luke shook his head dazedly. He scrubbed his hands across his burning, aching eyes. Joe Keller wouldn't lie to him—not good old Joe. It didn't make sense, what Joe was telling him. But Joe was so sure, then there must be something to it. Some miracle had happened. Either remorseless time had slowed, or distance had been compressed, somehow. For, out of the ashes of seemingly certain defeat, here was—victory!

He'd have to think—have to try and figure this out. But not now. He was too damn tired to think or figure anything. His brain was an unresponsive lump in a numbed head. All he could do was blink and stare.

Bonfires were springing up everywhere and multi-colored fireworks were going off, whooshing across the sky. A lot of strange people were all about, laughing, talking, yelling—putting on a wild celebration. People from Castle Mountain, they must be. Against the light of the various bonfires, Luke saw Johnny Megarry and Casey O'Keefe—saw Dick Leslie and the worn, haggard, still bewildered stalwarts of the construction gangs. They were all being lionized by the townfolk of Castle Mountain. They were being plied with hot coffee and cake and pie and all manner of food and refreshment. Somewhere a woman with a high, sweet voice began singing the 'Star-Spangled Banner.' What had been but a few moments before a bitter, dogged, brutal fight against time and distance had now become a midnight picnic and a celebration.

Of a sudden there was just one person Luke wanted to see. Dale Leslie. Where was she? He'd have to find her. For if victory was truly won, and it seemed that it must be, then it was at her feet that he wanted to lay the wreath. He blundered about, dead on his feet, trying to find her.

But they wouldn't let him find her. They were leading him up the gulch to town. Frank Ames and Curt Leffingwell were. 'Dale,' mumbled Luke. 'Dale—I've got to find Dale.'

'Don't you worry about that grand girl, Luke,' said Frank Ames. 'My wife is taking care of her as fondly as if the girl were her own daughter. Dale Leslie and the future will keep. Right now you've got to have some rest.'

They led him into a building and to a bed.

They pushed him down on that bed and Curt Leffingwell held a bottle to his lips. 'Take a snort, Luke,' he ordered. 'Take a big snort. It will relax you, let you sleep.'

The liquor burned in his throat, sent a warm tide through him, to soften up the brittle tautness of his nerves, loosen the knotted tenseness of his muscles. He lay back and closed his eyes. Sleep hit him like a massive club.

Frank Ames and Curt Leffingwell pulled off his boots, covered him with blankets. They moved quietly out, closing the door behind them. Frank Ames said, 'It would all be perfect, Curt—if only John Guthrie were here.'

Leffingwell nodded. 'That new engine we are ordering, Frank. The day it starts its initial run from Garnet, that name will be on it. The John B. Guthrie. And that name will roll back and forth over our road as long as a yard of steel remains.'

* * *

They sat in Frank Ames' office. Luke Fenimore, Ames, and Curt Leffingwell. Shaved, bathed and in fresh clothes, Luke looked much his old self, for thirty solid hours of sleep had replenished the wells of vigor.

Frank Ames was talking. 'Miss Leslie came to see me. Up here Curt and I knew something

234

of the great try you and your men were making, Luke. We would have liked to help, but there seemed nothing we could do except keep out of the way. We knew the steel was there, and the cross ties and all of the other supplies. So, all we could do was sit here and pull for you. And then came Miss Leslie, bringing us word of the great tragedy. That floored Curt and me, left us useless and whipped and unable even to think.

'But that grand girl brought something with her besides word of the crushing loss of John Guthrie, and of the blowing of Number Four. She brought an idea—a wonderful idea. Which was that we extend the town limits to meet you—to extend them as far as was reasonably possible. It was as simple as that. Senator Ring agreed to an extension of a quarter of a mile. That's the story. It meant all the difference between winning and losing.'

'I wish Miss Leslie were here now,' said Curt Leffingwell. 'I'd like to thank her again. But Frank tells me that she and her brother went back to Rancheria Flat yesterday afternoon.'

Luke had sat quietly, listening, his eyes grave. Now he stirred. 'There's still a lot of unfinished business,' he said grimly. 'There's Number Four bridge to be rebuilt. There's the final stretch of track up the flats to be graded and ballasted. For that matter, the entire road in from Garnet needs going over before it will

235

be in perfect shape. But we've got all summer to take care of that. The thing I'm mainly interested in right now is getting Henry Shard's hide. For he is just as guilty of murder as were those who actually shot John Guthrie and Flick Lee.' Frank Ames and Curt Leffingwell exchanged glances. Leffingwell took a short turn up and down the office. 'You can forget Henry Shard, Luke,' he said quietly. 'Henry Shard is dead.'

'Dead!' Luke's head jerked up.

Curt Leffingwell nodded. 'At the meeting where the extension of the town limits was voted, I told Shard what Frank and I intended to do; that we were going to swear out a warrant for his arrest, charging him with complicity in murder, among other things. He looked like a trapped rat. News of Bart Runnell's death seemed to floor him, too. At any rate, so the word goes, he went back to his office and locked himself in. You and your men won your fight at seven minutes to midnight. You remember the celebration that took place. Henry Shard must have heard that celebration and realized what it meant—that we had won and he had lost, all around. So, right after midnight, Shard shot himself. A miner, passing Shard's office, heard the shot.'

Luke got up, walked to a window and stood there for a time. 'So that's that,' he murmured. He turned. 'Now we can get back to work.'

'Not right away,' said Curt Leffingwell. 'I

don't want to hear of a single lick of work being done by you or any of the men for the next week, Luke. It's to be vacation for all hands—with full pay. And you, of course, are General Superintendent now.'

'No,' said Luke quietly. 'Not under that title, Curt. There was only one General Superintendent. And he is gone.'

Frank Ames produced bottle and glasses. 'We will drink to him, Luke. To John Guthrie!'

Luke lifted his glass. 'To John Guthrie. And to Flick Lee. I'll be a better man for having known both of them.'

* * *

Luke walked down the street and out of town and on toward the flats, where the Union Foundry engine was beginning to hiss and blow under a full head of steam. There were several flats hooked on and men of the gangs were gathered round about. They too had slept the stupor of utter, complete weariness away and were bright and quick and full of vitality again.

Casey O'Keefe leaned from the window of his cab and yelled, 'We've been waitin' for you, Luke. The boys want to see what Rancheria Flat looks like again.'

'No need stopping there, Casey,' answered Luke. 'For it's a week's vacation for all hands, with full pay. After that we go back to work and polish up the job.'

237

Which brought a cheer.

They weaved and clanked and lurched along. Here and there as they passed some spot that had been particularly tough going, the men would point to it and discuss it. Their heads were up and pride was in every eye. Here was a tale to tell in the bunkhouses of future jobs, a tale that would make them members of a select brotherhood. Forgotten were the racking hours of toil and sleeplessness and dogged punishment. That was all behind them, now. Here, before their very eyes, on the rails and ties over which they rode, lay the proof of what they had done. Here was their victory, won against impossible odds. And they savored it to the full, and were content.

There was a short stop at Rancheria Flat. There were odds and ends of clothing and belongings the men wanted to gather up and take with them on their holiday. At the Flat it was Keno Udell who sidled up to Luke and drawled, 'That Miss Dale, she sure sits a saddle plumb handsome, I couldn't help but think of what a picture she made when she pulled out for Cold Creek, first thing this morning.'

Luke looked down at the little man, smiling. 'You don't miss a cussed thing, do you, Keno?'

Keno's eyes twinkled. 'Habit of mine, Luke—lookin' and seein'.'

They rolled on to Cold Creek. Luke

stopped in at Ma Megarry's and found Dick Leslie waiting there. Luke grinned at him. 'Well, kid—it was a rocky ride, wasn't it? But we managed to nose in under the wire, thanks to Dale.'

'Still a lot to do,' said Dick. 'I'm going to get right at the rebuilding of Number Four. I want your permission to go out to Garnet and pick out the timbers I'll need.'

Luke waved a hand. 'You're to do nothing for the next week, same as the rest of us. Orders from Frank Ames and Curt Leffingwell. It's vacation with pay for all hands.'

'You heard about Henry Shard?' asked Dick soberly.

Luke nodded. 'There are always some like that. They can hand it out, but they can't take it. Well, we've things to remember and things to forget. I hope your sister will be able to forget some of those things.'

'Such as?'

'Bart Runnell,' said Luke slowly. 'Why he died and how he died.'

'Sis is quite a remarkable person,' said Dick quietly. 'Just how remarkable I never quite realized until the past few days. She has a pretty strict code. A person either measures up with Sis, or they don't. They're right or they're wrong—there's none of this halfway business. So, though she's never breathed a word of how she felt to me, I realize now that she long ago

239

crossed out the name of Bart Runnell. Remember the day you and I were discussing her and Runnell and I was worried? Well, you said then that we could trust Dale's judgment, that if Runnell was what we thought he was, she'd see through him. You were right, Luke. And Sis was never morbid-minded. Things to be forgotten, she'll forget.'

'I'm glad to hear you say that, Dick,' Luke said. 'I feel better. About Number Four, you've got a free hand, of course. Go where you want, get what you need. But not for a week, understand?'

Dick stretched his arms, grinned boyishly. 'Yessir, Boss. Just as you say.' Dick was whistling as he went out.

Luke hung about his room for a time, restless as a caged panther. Several times he went to the window and looked out across town to where the Leslie cabin stood. A deepening eagerness grew in him. Finally he could stand it no longer. This was something he had to know about, one way or the other.

The cabin was quiet when he came up to it, but when he knocked it was Dale who opened the door. She was her old self again, cool and immaculate in fresh-pressed gingham. Her lovely eyes were clear and direct, yet soft with inner musings.

'Hello Luke,' she said.

Luke thought of the other times he had stood in this room. 'I've been pretty rough at

240

times, I'm afraid,' he said. 'I'm sorry, Dale—about Bart Runnell. I'm sorry for the way I reported his death to you. That was nothing less than brutal.'

'We've both been brutal at times, Luke,' was her grave reply. 'There was a night, just outside this door, when I was guilty.'

He knew the night she meant—the night she had blazed at him, telling him she hated him, would always hate him.

'Maybe I had that coming, Dale.'

'No! No, you didn't. I've realized since that it was myself I hated, because I was trying to make myself believe things that I knew were lies.' She hesitated, then went on, superbly honest. 'And I was hating Bart Runnell, because you were all the things he should have been but wasn't. It isn't very pretty to hear a woman speak of hate, is it?'

'Why not? It can be an honest emotion. So there are a lot of things finished.'

She nodded. 'Finished and forgotten. Agreed?'

'Agreed. Dick was quite right when he said you were a very remarkable person. An opinion shared by every man who took part in the big job. We won because of your spirit and faith and longheadedness.'

'Nonsense!' she scoffed, but it was gentle scoffing. 'We won because no group of men ever toiled so terribly, so wonderfully. You and your men built that railroad, Luke—no others.'

Luke smiled gravely. 'I could argue with you there, but I didn't come here to argue. I came to tell you that I love you, Dale.'

She went very still, so still that Luke thought he had overstepped. He went on doggedly.

'I came to tell you there has never been anyone else who counted, except you. I knew that the very first day I ever set eyes on you, that day when we were coming in from Garnet in the caboose. I guess I'm not saying it very well, am I?'

Her laugh was soft, her eyes and lips suddenly very tender. 'I think you are saying it wonderfully, Luke.'

She came into his arms, as definitely honest and straightforward as she had always been.